SILENCES, OR A WOMAN'S LIFE

ALSO BY MARIE CHAIX
IN ENGLISH TRANSLATION

The Laurels Of Lake Constance

SILENCES, OR A WOMAN'S LIFE

MARIE CHAIX

TRANSLATED BY HARRY MATHEWS

DALKEY ARCHIVE PRESS
CHAMPAIGN / LONDON / DUBLIN

Originally published in French as *Les silences ou la vie d'une femme* by Éditions du Seuil, Paris, 1976

First edition, 2012

Chaix, Marie, 1942-
[Silences, ou la vie d'une femme. English]
Silences, or a woman's life / Marie Chaix ; translated by Harry Mathews. -- 1st ed.
p. cm.
ISBN 978-1-56478-795-8 (pbk. : acid-free paper)
1. Coma--Patients--Fiction 2. Mothers and daughters--Fiction. I. Mathews, Harry, 1930- II. Title.
PQ2663.H259S513 2012
843'.914--dc23
2012033090

Partially funded by a grant from the Illinois Arts Council, a state agency

Cet ouvrage a bénéficié du soutien des Programmes d'aide à la publication de l'Institut français/ministère français des affaires étrangères et européennes

This work was supported by the Publications Assistance Programs of the French Institute / French Ministry of Foreign and European Affairs

www.dalkeyarchive.com

Cover: design and composition by Sarah French

Printed on permanent/durable acid-free paper and bound in the United States of America

for Anne

"What will be left of me?

"What legacy of childhood sorrows, of wasted tears, of wars misunderstood and freedom misused, of unflagging love, and times of mourning, and unfulfilled dreams—what legacy of sleep and forgetfulness shall I bequeath to time, which will forget me as well?"

I encountered her by chance one day, between bare museum walls, and I recognized her at once. I wasn't surprised. She sat there, motionless in her gloomy surroundings, as if she had been expecting me for years. I went up to her. Gradually the white walls around us faded away, and I saw her in the dull glow of the floor lamp that stood beside her.

On the floor lies a coarse rug. It might be threadbare, with its weft and soiled edges plain to see; it might be decorated with timeworn flowers; or not. Its texture hardly matters, or how old and shabby it has become, because it is simply ageless. Its washed-out colors have merged into one indefinable hue—a mauve-gray, a musty purple, a brownish green: the color of dust and old age that you can smell in all the places where old people live, where for decades nothing has changed. On the rug, a stool littered with bits of old cloth; next to it, a battered wicker sewing basket trailing tangled embroidery threads; on a stand covered in crumpled lace, an oval silver-plate box (its lid of enamel or marble) that once contained who knows what—perhaps sweets stuck together, gumdrops, or candied violets; or sugared almonds from some half-forgotten baptism; or rusty hairpins? Behind the box stand seven frames of varying size, of which some are gilt, the rest black and chipped. Within them, stained and faded, family snapshots gleam faintly: a smiling couple, a vigorous-looking soldier, a beaming baby, a group of sickly children with a flowering thicket behind them, a dignified old mother. In front of them lies a pair of steel-rimmed spectacles.

In the uncertain light of the floor lamp (its long uneven fringe of dirty string was once embellished with glass beads), in this harsh intimacy without windows or daylight, she sits in a massive armchair of brown wood: the image of a woman and of a life that are drawing to their close.

From her waxy oilcloth dress, patterned with floral green and violet, four stiff white limbs emerge. They are bones—not those of a human skeleton but crude animal remains that could as well be worn, whitened branches that the winter sea casts up on the shore. The ones that represent her legs stand upright in the large laced black shoes, which have apparently been deformed by some chronic infirmity. The hands are realistic—rheumatic plaster gloves, one gripping the armrest next to a cane that leans against the chair, the other tightly clutching a fat gray cat that lies nestled against an unimaginable belly. The cat's eyes are appalling: pitiless and full of spite, as if they had soaked up all the force of hate and resentment accumulated during a life of regrets.

The woman's head is a large jar, tilted onto its side so that its base displays her face—the sweet face of a young woman, enclosed in a finely wrought gilt frame. When the jar is seen in profile, however, glass eyes stare out from a fleshless skull (a rabbit's perhaps, or a sheep's). Her shoulders and bosom have disappeared beneath a tangle of jars. The point of this strange decoration is not at once apparent, but a closer look reveals that what she is wearing around her neck is her life. It's as though her translucent skull had been drained of all remembrance, and her memories had been gathered in these little jars that cling to her, strung together by slender chains to form a ghastly necklace. The jars contain outdated images of old joys and sorrows: the recollections, enhanced by time and forgetfulness, which give a life its value and which, when that life is spent, are no more than dead objects to the people who inherit them. Medallions, crucifixes, locks of hair, amulets, feathers, pebbles, dried flowers, insects . . . They cling to her old age like venerable keepsakes; she has put them in chains for fear of losing them. The head is empty, but the images remain, under glass. And everything stays where it belongs.

A simple background completes the setting of this declining life: a partition of varnished mahogany set waist-high behind the chair, underneath a bedstead covered in a yellowing flowered cretonne. At the center of the bedstead, in an oval frame, reigns a life-sized portrait of the husband, the man, the dear departed, with his medals and his mustache.

And there she waits, waits, waits—she has been entitled *The Wait* (by the sculptor Kienholz, her creator). In the desolation of her invalid's immobility, what is there to wait for besides the definitive immobility that will be neither more nor less horrifying? It will not modify her setting (her dead and buried past), it will not change her in other people's eyes—they go their way and forget her.

That day in the museum I could hardly tear myself away from the worn rug or the wan light that cast shadows round the woman in the chair. I almost sat down on the stool to talk to her, but the cat gave me a dirty look. It was time to leave.

Night was falling. It was the appointed hour for my visit. She would be waiting for me, seated in the yellow light of the floor lamp, with her glasses on her nose and the little chains that secured them quivering against her cheeks. She would be knitting, or embroidering a doily, with the cat on her lap; or perhaps watching television, with one ear cocked for my footsteps outside the door and the ringing of the doorbell.

There was a woman in my life whom I loved. Until now, I had limited my thoughts to the moments of happiness that my visits gave her.

Had I so readily accepted her condition of invalid, of seated woman, that only the loveliness of her face still spoke to me and made me forget her age? Had I, out of discretion or anxiety, locked her face inside a frame and strung memories around her neck so that they were all I saw, so that I could hide her true likeness, that of a woman nearing her end?

Now I had met her double; and old age had abruptly started looking like death.

I went to see her often. Sometimes I would tell her in advance, sometimes not. She was always expecting me, seated in her armchair. Listening for the sound of the elevator, she would have Juliette open the door before I'd had time to ring. I was careful never to catch her unprepared. In the corridor I would slowly take off my coat and fix my hair, while Juliette, in a few innocuous sentences, submitted her report—about the weather, the day's meals, which medicines had been taken and which refused, what was being shown on television, whether the night had been calm or beset by dreams, and what kind of dreams: the daily routine of two solitary women.

She liked hearing my voice before she saw me. She could then cry out from where she sat, "Oh, it's you." As if there could be any doubt about that.

I went into the living room. By the time my eyes met hers, she had time to put away her knitting, set her glasses down on the little table, and smooth back her hair with one hand. She would look up at me and smile; take my hands, one at a time; pull me toward her, and breathe in my scent as she kissed me. She needed to touch and smell. I was the whole outside world—life, animation, the winds, the city streets. I was a happening whose very essence she longed to extract, so that she could emerge from her lethargy and, for an instant, be restored to the life that other people lead, the life that eluded her, doomed as she was to the confines of her infirmity, like a still life in its frame—"*Stilleben*," she would say in self-mockery. "I'm nothing but a *Stilleben*," mingling German with her French, as she often did, especially since her accident.

It was true that, seen from a distance, settled in the living room with the tapestry and the unopened piano in the background, she recalled some antique painting of a Rhenish queen whose reign was nearing its end—a pale face in a cloud of blonde ruffles—or the portrait of the artist's wife eking out her old age in a dim Flemish interior: a picture like the ones that follow you as you pass the ill-lighted anterooms of a museum. But when you drew nearer, the light from within her eyes illuminated the whole scene.

She used to say: "When you're here, it's brighter and warmer. My old wheels start turning—look, I'm actually moving!"

Ten years of partial paralysis had subjected her to a pitiless apprenticeship of immobility, but they had taught her as well the art of movement. None of her gestures was haphazard. She was aware of the slightest blink of her eyelids, of the smallest arc her good arm described. It was a feat to drink a cup of tea without spilling a drop. To follow an entire conversation and respond to every question demanded of her a concentration that only her infinite pride could disguise as easygoing urbanity. Her liveliest moments were thus for her the most exhausting. But she let nothing show—at most a flush would redden her brow or a sigh escape her lips. If anyone tried to assist her in finishing a sentence or disentangling the strands of her yarn, she became irritable. The impudence of being offered a helping hand made her furious. "Having a cane is quite enough," she would mutter, clutching the armrest of her chair.

She wasn't all that old. She was at that precarious age that made others say, with the slightest hint of cruelty, "How beautiful she must have been!" It was the age when everything starts slowing down, even if you refuse to admit it, when past life matters more than what lies ahead. One thing seems sure: the best is behind you. To go on living with a smile means inventing a whole new set of demands on oneself.

The age when hair turns white . . . Some women find it comforting; it makes them more beautiful. They're the ones whose busy, well-filled lives have manifestly followed the rhythm of the seasons, unchecked by heat, frost, or bad weather. Their lives may not always have been rosy, but these have left no more trace on their faces than a butterfly on a windowpane: white-haired ladies whose smooth skin and bright glances reassure us. You can imagine them experiencing one great love: bearing children whom they teach to survive the years by accepting joys and avoiding crises; contemplating at present their excited or tearful or rambunctious grandchildren; as though it were normal for successive generations to move from inevitable wars to times of grace, from stirring infatuations to sorrows that will be forgotten. When you see them, slow-moving and serene in their haloes of white locks, you take heart, and you tell yourself that growing old isn't perhaps so terrible after all.

But usually you glimpse these old ladies in the street, or, when you're little, emerging from church with lace shawls over their heads; or you look for them in photograph albums where you can barely make them out in the yellowing prints. It's rare that you know any of them. More likely you will fondly imagine them, some melancholy day when you discover in your mirror a white hair in the midst of the brown, or when a tiny line appears at the corner of your eye or mouth.

She would have enjoyed being a quiet, proud old lady, with a little black silk ribbon around her neck—the kind you read about in novels, the kind whose beauty is enhanced by their great age. How often did I hear her say, "If I can still be myself, I don't mind growing old. But if I get to be ugly—kill me!" That was in the days when we all used to laugh at her fastidiousness, when there was no evident threat to her vigor. Now age has duped her by making each year count double. There had been no more joking about a future tinged with the violet light of melancholy. The question was how to disguise the present, now that her fast-dwindling powers were so hard put to withstand its gray injustice.

She had held her own nevertheless. She still was beautiful. Her unblemished face showed no signs of her terrible infirmity or of the ordeals that had affected her so cruelly. It seemed ageless because it reflected simultaneously all the stages of her life. You might glimpse the adolescent or the little girl through the transitory mask of the full-grown woman or the woman in love—a disturbing, ever-changing image, like the curious snapshots produced by double exposure that show several pictures superimposed. The pale green eyes that imparted to her face a translucency of stained glass seemed to beg forgiveness for having kept their limpid youthfulness, for shedding on time and objects a light undimmed by the slightest regret. "Believe it or not," they said, "I'm still here, and I'm hanging on." I sometimes forgot that there was more to her than her face.

Of late she didn't stir from her chair. I would kiss her, then congratulate her on her looks or the harmonious colors of her clothes (helped by her housekeeper, she took inordinate pains with her dress, showing a predilection for mauve, for muslin scarves and soft wools). At last I would sit down on the stool covered in the same cross-stitching as her chair and lay my hands open on her lap. On them she would place her own left hand, on which scattered spots seemed woven into a mitt of beige lace.

She would turn her head toward the window and, not looking at me, casually remark, "It would be nice to go out with you for a little walk, but it's a little chilly, don't you think?"

I would bend nearer her hand, caressing the blue path of her veins with the tip of my forefinger, and answer in a most natural tone, "It's much warmer here, we'll have plenty of time for walking some other day," thinking all the while of the effort she would make a little later, when, leaning on Juliette and on her cane, she took me to the door.

When she wasn't tired, we would talk at great length, about everything and nothing, above all about the past. A dream she'd had, or a news item on the radio, or three notes of a concerto would momentarily bring back to her an episode whose details she conscientiously described to me in a carefully chosen vocabulary. She was afraid of losing her memory, of no longer finding her words. Each story was an exercise for her. "I'm giving my head a workout," she'd say with a laugh—proof that not all her gears had jammed.

To illustrate her tales, she made me fetch albums from the cupboard, or else with her cane pointed out on the wall in front of her a portrait, a family gathering, or some other framed relic: a child's drawing, a certificate of confirmation. Often, in the middle of a sentence or at the turning point of a situation she was minutely describing, she would stop, as though an obstacle had abruptly and unexpectedly fallen across her path. She would cast a quick imploring look at me, her eyes would go gray and distant, she would run her hand over her forehead and shake her head, and then begin a sweeping gesture as if to dispel a cloud of smoke. I would grasp her hand as it fluttered through the air, and she would smile at me gratefully.

"I've lost it," she would breathlessly declare, "it's vanished. What were we talking about?"

I would quickly invent some silly thing to tell her. Not hearing what I said, she would laugh, for my sake. Then, knowing how reluctant I always was to leave, she would exclaim with a conspicuous glance at the watch she no longer ever wore, "Oh, my, how late it is! You've got to be going."

I would help her to her feet and hand her her cane, which she gripped with a look of rage. She quickly restored a smile to her briefly straitened features, then started forward and saw me to the door, lurching all the way. I avoided paying attention to how she walked or making any gesture that might let her think I had doubts about her absolute self-sufficiency. Leaning against the doorjamb, she watched me ring for the elevator and, as I disappeared behind the sliding door, blew me a kiss.

This parting glimpse of her was as upsetting to me as a reproach. I was abandoning her to dark walls covered with pictures, photographs, and bound books she would never again open; to a confined universe cluttered with massive pieces of furniture that had become way stations of her unvarying round between armchair and door; to her lace and the lamps with their veined lampshades of imitation parchment and the doilies that formed her surroundings. I could imagine her slumping back into her chair, cursing her cane as she put it away, settling for two minutes (or ten, or more) into a morose contemplation of the wall. She'd inspect all of them, each in his frame—the dead, the living, the missing, the dearly loved ones: mute witnesses of a halted life, discreet ghosts come to haunt her muffled solitude and remind her incessantly that there was nothing they could do about it. Then she would come back to herself, shivering, drawing the fringed shawl across her bosom; shrugging her shoulders, picking up her spectacles, and concentrating once more on her knitting—the one occupation (along with embroidery) that she could satisfactorily manage left-handed, with a needle held fast in an elastic strap slipped over the wrist of her paralyzed right hand.

Anyone who hadn't known her "before" and who saw her for the first time after she had become (as she liked to say) a "professional invalid" had a hard time imagining what her life had been like. Often enough, age leaves faces cruelly stamped with marks of behavior, accident, or simply the passage of the years. This is why studying an unfamiliar face is so fascinating: the features are shaped according to a formula mysteriously suited to each individual, according to a subterranean progress whose reflection, as it blooms or withers, becomes the "expression" of that face, tinged variously with sorrow, boredom, resignation, or discouragement, or, on the contrary, with vitality, gaiety, and optimism. An aging face is a pathetic appeal uttered unawares by someone's past experience. Show me your wrinkles, your wounds, and the circles under your eyes, and I may start learning who you were.

Her face provided few clues. Through what miracle, through what special dispensation of time had it preserved the invulnerability of a sensible, smiling statue? She had her secrets; but her vanity was boundless. It was hard to believe the pleasure she took in misleading her occasional visitors. She would deploy a subtle charm, all restraint, sweetness, and warmth, soothing glances and words. People went away astonished, without a thought for her faltering gestures and fettered body. "The woman has probably suffered, but something like grace has seen her though" is what they would be thinking, remembering only the brightness of her clear gaze, whose liquid placidity perfectly concealed the rugged terrain that had taken what seemed like centuries to traverse.

Her old age had caught us unprepared. One day when she was still youthful, something—perhaps some grief too intense to be borne—made her stumble and, for many a long day, go blank. "Coma" was the medical term for this passage through the land of mists. Against every expectation, the sleeper then came back to life—a life on which she opened her eyes without recognizing it. Henceforth she would walk with a cane; she would never again run her fingers over the keys—oh, everything she now would lack was too much to take in at a glance. But she would have plenty of time to think about it, now that she was old.

In a matter of days—for her, countless centuries of sleep—she had gone to the end of the bleak sunset path where people usually adopt successive disguises, planning stops along the way so as to ultimately get used to the imperceptible changes that from year to year transform them into other people.

She woke up from her journey tired and wobbly, astonished at having become that "someone else," that person on the far side of things, on the downhill side of things, the nebulous ghost that waits for each of us someplace else, farther on, later, but inescapably there, with white hair, sunken eyes, slow gestures, the shawl worn all year round.

For a long time she refused to look in a mirror. She would mumble, "What do I look like? What's happening? Half my face feels like marble." Did she sometimes think, "Better not to have woken up"?

She never let on. To all appearances, she was ready to play her new role of dignified old lady without a murmur.

Having known her "before," I still saw her youth amid the marks of age. Two women walked together on the frontiers of dream, sometimes losing sight of one another, sometimes reuniting and merging into one. In the depths of her unaltered gaze and grave voice, she fitfully summoned up the memory of the woman who had deserted her body but now sprang forth, obscurely and fortuitously, in the glint of a green eye or the lilting sparkle of her words.

For a long time, sheltered by her glance, I did not see that she was growing old. It was no doubt to protect myself from the grief I felt at her sudden illness that, with her help, I learned overnight to love another woman; noticing, it's true, how spent her gestures and how slow her movements had become, but interpreting this as a role she had ingeniously contrived, an artful stratagem that allowed her to conceal whatever it was in her that had lost its vigor.

The tapestries, the woodwork, the jumble of cloth that surrounded her formed an enclave untouched by the city and by time, a place where an ageless woman on the fringe of things was living an unreal old age. The doctors—they always knew best—said that normally she should have succumbed to her attack. And yet here she was, a goddess of pearl-embroidered velvet, living out a present that would have been denied her if she hadn't hung on to it with every ounce of her strength, constructing and reconstructing a past that she did not blame for having abandoned her.

Then one night, a city night like any other, it happens. Later you think: you weren't expecting it but you needn't have been surprised. By then it's too late: it's already happened. A moment when the threads that hold a life together loosen and stretch and split and are left dangling. There is nothing to be held together now, no days to be linked to other days, nothing to be collected and clung to. The knot forgets to reknot itself and sunders. It's the conclusion to a long story

That's all there was to it. On a mild autumn night, a night when you light up a cigarette after the movies on your way home to listen to Mahler's Fifth; on an October evening when you leave your windows open on the horse-chestnut trees (now shedding their plumage); on an evening when you're not expecting it, it happens. The phone rings. You don't like hearing the phone ring at night; but after all, it may be a wrong number. Juliette's voice sounds unnatural:

"Come over. Come over right away. Something's gone wrong. Why weren't you here? How could you go to the movies just when . . . ! Come over right away, something's gone wrong."

It was the right number after all. That evening I had felt engulfed by the city, safe from anything unexpected. But it's here, I've been found out, there's no escape. I begin an interminable descent, sliding down a slippery rope without any knots to break my fall.

I'll take my time. Since she didn't wait for me before taking flight or warn me that the time for her departure had come, she can wait now. Time enough for the sluggish flow running up and down my nerves and paralyzing me to withdraw and let me walk again; for the far-off gray swell to reach, overwhelm, and drown me; time for me to realize that this night, let's face it, is not a night like any other, that now you—you too, but why must it be you?—have become someone I shall have to usher to the gate of the stone garden.

Only a few blocks separate my place from hers. I walk them slowly, drinking in the darkness, making it last, inching along like someone afraid of arriving early at an appointment made long before. We'll meet again somewhere, you and I, under an unknown sky. Neither of us will be the same. I'm practicing a mute language that will communicate with your silence. I want to be indifferent and look at you without trembling. I'm creating a void inside me that gets colder and more intoxicating with each gulp of darkness, with each step that brings me closer to you. This void, weighty as a suit of armor, is the one guarantee of my strength. (Something's gone wrong. Of course something's gone wrong. Something was bound to go wrong. We knew that. We'd been told that. Miracles don't happen.) I stop. Ridiculous words start assailing my throat. I try inhaling cigarette smoke to keep them down. I'm babbling. Keep calm. Keep moving. Only one short block to go.

Something has certainly gone wrong. Things have been going wrong for ages now. "She's living on borrowed time" was what they said. I'd been hearing that for ten years. I'd grown accustomed to this shadow-woman, to this frail survivor of a collapse that had cost her half of her self; accustomed to the slowing down of her entire being—that was how she kept going, it seemed, eking out her life at her own pace. Her gestures may have been clumsy, but in every instance they were planned and evaluated ahead of time. Her mind may have been in some way unsettled, but it manifested a fierce and unshakable longing to not lose control. And those eyes: blurry, then emerging from their misty pools to follow the other person's least utterance and gesture, not missing a thing, and then missing the point of the story, the most obvious attitude, drifting off again, eyes now foundering and crying out for help. And that voice of hers, a little faint, cautiously articulating its words lest they be mistakenly shunted into inappropriate sentences by her disobedient brain; words repeated again and again, forced out in spite of her impatience: "Wait, I've lost track, you're going too fast—please, start at the beginning." Her ponderous, shuffling steps, dependent on the stability of a cane (you who were so erect and proud and beautiful!), a pathetic staff that she tried to forget by leaving it in corners or behind the curtains ("Juliette! Where did you hide my cane this time?")—maintaining the illusion, as long as she remained seated, that she might get up by herself and start walking. How did I manage to accept her slowness, her lurching, her falls, the tears she held back, the formidable courage demanded of her by every passing minute? How did I manage, until tonight, to watch her living between parentheses?

Startled by my approach, a black cat concealed by a garbage can jumps out of a pile of litter and streaks across the sidewalk in front of me. She'd always said that this meant bad luck. It was something she'd learned from her grandmother's grotesque behavior whenever a black cat provoked her in this fashion. She would let out a shriek, tightly shut her eyes, cross herself, and, in a swirl of starched petticoats, turn around three times wherever she happened to be standing. All of a sudden I can't go on. It's stupid, but the black cat has reminded me of a gray one and a dark association of images makes me flop down on a bench between a row of overturned garbage cans and a foul-smelling outdoor urinal. The questionable charm of my surroundings scarcely bothers me. This is no place or time for daydreaming, but I've been turned to paper, rags, sawdust, succumbing to the nightmare that has so often entered my waking hours since Kienholz's merciless revelation provided me with the images of a reality I was incapable of mastering. Tonight, as I sit on Rue de la Convention and stare at a depressing hospital wall, she looms in front of me with a gray cat on her lap . . .

I'm afraid. Afraid of opening the door and finding her immobilized in her chair, turned to stone inside her waxy tatters, one hand clutching the cat, the other crushing her glasses. Afraid of a muddied glass eye in its white socket, of the orthopedic shoes permanently glued to marble feet, of the useless spools of cotton spilling out of a sewing basket. Afraid because she is no longer waiting for me. Where are you? Why are you abandoning me to the bony ghost that keeps haunting me?

Stop. Imagine a different scene. Get up off the bench and start running. I get up and start running. I needn't be so sure—I haven't seen what's happened yet. Maybe it's just a plain dizzy spell. Juliette has fits over nothing. Ten years of struggle. Why precisely tonight—on such a mild night—would she decide to play tricks on me?

Running is warming me up. My steps clatter and resound in the sleeping street. I'm already laughing about it. In a while we'll be laughing together. I'll pass her a glass of water with a few multicolored pills cupped in my hand to make her feel absolutely fine. Drawing a shawl over her breast, she'll say to me, "You shouldn't have bothered. You know I have my little weak spells, but I get over them. Now it's time to go to bed." I'll breathe in the downy scent of her powdered cheek against my cheek, and tomorrow everything will go on as usual.

I've reached the door of her building. I ring. The railing voice on the interphone makes me jump: "Finally! You sure took your time." Took my time? But I've been running. I'm here. The door swings open with a long squeak. Quick, get inside and see her. Juliette rushes up to me. My head starts spinning.

"Everything was going fine, we were watching television after dinner . . ." What I see is the slant-backed empty armchair; the flowered curtains are drawn; her unhidden cane against the armrest. "The cat was asleep on the table. We'd had a cup of chamomile tea. The program didn't interest her, although it did me. 'Juliette, pass me my knitting.' Then, you see, I saved two stitches for her . . ." What I see is her workbox on the floor by the chair, and strands of colored wool untidily spilling out of it; her glasses have been placed on the stand.

"We hadn't been talking; and then she said to me in a funny voice, 'I'm through with this. It's finished.' 'But, Madame, you're hardly started it,' and she was stopping, you understand, she was stopping—look!" I see the photographs on the wall over the piano; there they are, all of them, with their gilt frames and fixed smiles, their gestures frozen on one particular day in their lives. "So I knew something had gone wrong. It was hard getting her to her room and helping her undress. She did what I told her to, like a robot. She didn't say another word to me. She's been asleep ever since—well, come and see."

I sit down instead. The cat jumps onto my lap and settles there, purring, kneading my skin with almost clawless paws. I don't stop him and I stroke the gray back undulating beneath my fingers. Crossing her arms, Juliette paces around the table. "This time, you know—this time . . ." and she starts telling me what happened again from the beginning. By repeating her words she is trying to gain some understanding of what is awry in the situation. She's irritating me. I'd like to understand, too, quietly and coolly. I'd like to find an explanation simple enough for us to grasp. To reassure us.

"Stop walking around like that, you're making me dizzy. She's asleep? If she's asleep, it can't be too serious."

(A shrug of the shoulders.)

"You don't understand a thing. First of all, there's the knitting. It's crazy, all those unfinished stitches."

"That's true—the knitting. That's it. That's the whole problem. Tell me again what happened with the knitting."

She hands me the unfinished work. Her tight-lipped expression chides my foolishness, my slowness in accepting a story that she already knows by heart. She watches me turn the woolen square over and over. A strand hangs from one of its corners—I give it a yank, and a ball of yarn tumbles out of the basket. The cat sits up on my lap and jumps on the ball.

I can see her bent over the knitting needles. Her glasses have slipped down her nose. She hasn't gotten very far with her work, three stripes of different colors—her first scarf of the winter. She's making laborious headway—knit one, purl one; she straightens up from time to time to look blankly at the television screen. She takes a slightly longer break, shutting her eyes, shaking her head, trying to get rid of the stiffness invading her neck. Nothing serious, she knows, something that comes and goes. The sound of the television set suddenly starts hurting her behind the eyes, piercing her forehead like bright flashes of a neon sign—she wants to ask Juliette to stop the awful racket but the words are stuck in her cheeks. Something thick is rising in her throat and weighing down the bones of her jaw. Abruptly she turns into a fly: her big, multifaceted eyes can distinguish every fiber of the wool. She's frightened. She wants to call out but can't. Fly legs are muddling the stitches, which fall off the needles with a limp mucky sound and form holes as big as wells—she's teetering on their edge. She's certain of one thing: she has no more time, she has to act fast and can't do it. She has to finish her stupid knitting and cry out for help. Juliette can't hear her, she's enthralled by the program. The cat's asleep. Why are these thousands of flies flitting now around her head, and this viscous stuff in her mouth that's so hard to swallow? At last Juliette turns around. Why is she shouting through a glass wall? "Madame! Madame!" She feels so, so far away, a little fly among flies. She starts blowing words through her proboscis, sticky bubbles floating in a fish tank: "Stop-this-knitting-it's-done." What a relief! Done. She's said done. It's done.

I can see the stitches linked one above the other, and the last three, wobbling little loops slipping off the needle as it falls to the floor with a metallic sound. The flies have taken off, preceding her in a humming cloud that congregates on the ceiling above the window. She follows them awkwardly, her buzzing wings grazing the shag of the curtain, and alights on the cold curtain rod. Up there, with her overall view of the room, she sees an old woman's ponderous body start moving like a stone statue ineffectually pushed forward, dragging itself down the corridor to her room, falling onto the bed and sinking into darkness.

(Borrowed time. Living, knitting, on borrowed time: ten years of it. Ten years knitting nonstop. Always a piece of work in progress, yarn to be bought, a perpetual knitting spree. One hand lifeless, its only use to hold down one tame needle under its weight of flesh; the other hand going like crazy, pulling the yarn, pushing the other needle back and forth, making loops and knots, working away till it cramps. Let's not waste time: knit and keep knitting. Scarves, coverlets, and lots of little patchwork squares, that's easier, you just follow a straight line, no decrease or increase. And bootees—lots of baby's bootees. Can't do anything else, so might as well keep knitting till your brain is snarled. Poor old brain anyway, it can't think anymore, it can't keep up. So keep knitting. It's your only hope. Ten years of it. It had to end sometime, didn't it? There. My dears, I've knitted you ten years of old age, and that's enough. This is my will and testament, these are my last woolen wishes. I can't write or speak anymore, so I bequeath you these few little patches to wrap your winter thoughts in. Good-bye.)

The cat has torn the ball of yarn to tatters. I cut the thread that connects it to the knitting and set it on the table.

"There's something else I should have told you," says Juliette with a cunning look. "Last night she had a nightmare. She heard a humming all around her, and when she turned on the light the walls were swarming with black flies. That's a bad sign, for sure. And another thing I forgot—she kept vomiting. She couldn't stop. Come and see."

Everything is getting clearer. No more time for pictures. I go to her room. She is lying on her back; she's breathing; her hair is strewn over the pillow. She's breathing: for the time being. Occasionally a mild spasm shakes her, but the vomiting has stopped. Her breathing is steady, the skin of her arm silky and warm. Under her nightgown her breast gently rises and falls to the beat of a heart that remains loyal to its husk and does its work gallantly; does whatever is necessary for life to be present, for blood to run through veins and give color to the skin—that silky, warm skin. Nothing, for the time being, has changed. All is calm.

"Everything's going fine, really. She's just asleep."

And I tiptoe out of the room. Juliette shrugs her shoulders and lifts her eyes to the ceiling. (The chandelier is truly hideous. Why is she so attached to that chandelier, with its teardrops and its dust-catching pendants? What melancholy hides behind these prongs of twisted metal fashioned into coarse ivy leaves and hanging all askew?)

"Whatever you say. Let's wait and see. But if you expect her to wake up fresh and pink tomorrow morning—"

That's it—we'll wait and see. Wait for what? Let's wait for the sake of waiting. Let's wait, all three of us, for day to break.

So now here I am sitting in your chair, amid your walls and relics. You're through with watching over a distant past that was crumbling in your memory, through with assembling scraps of life like ill-matching pieces in a puzzle where you would never recover your own likeness. You're tired of waiting; you've gone off without a word, leaving me to renew your patience. You've fallen asleep without warning, without complaining, but leaving no message. It's up to me to decipher your sleep and hear the sentences your silence speaks. Are you planning to desert this hostile body that you're sick of? Will you start moving in darkness back through all the nights of dreaming, waiting, and loneliness that have punctuated your life?

As you walked in your sleep, how many rooftops, peaks, and cliffs did you pass? From how many dreams were you woken up by sudden voids opening beneath your hesitant steps, by streams that all at once gushed forth and undermined your precarious path, by abrupt halts at the threshold of shattered bridges, leaving you to stare at an inaccessible shore whose riches turned to sand between your outstretched fingers?

As you teetered in your sleep along the ridge of your life, could you count the shocks that had hurt you? If only you could go your own free way at last, far from this broken body! If only you could take wing without hindrance, without being summoned back to the ways of the world, without waking up to days of which none were improvements!

I wish that this night that you've chosen for your excursion would stretch into infinity and that you could go on wandering peacefully among the hills of sleep. I don't want to give you up yet; I want to imagine your itinerary and follow you down the winding path of oblivion you have taken. If I must lose track of you, don't let it happen too fast. Give me time to bid your silhouette farewell as it falters on the rim of the horizon.

I'm waiting, and I have time to wait. Something in the color of this darkness, in the best of your pulse, something in the rhythm of your peaceful breathing and the stubborn convexity of your closed lids tells me not to expect you back. This time your sleep masks a real departure. But I'm not frightened. I'm keeping watch.

Soon, in the new morning, you will be already far away. I long to fall asleep at your side; but I have to get moving. I'm still one of the living, and we aren't allowed to go to sleep in the daytime and converse with a shadow. And the sad fact is that I'll have to call them to your bedside. They'll come on the run.

They won't realize it, but I'll be leading parallel lives: a visible life, in which I'll follow your body wherever they decide to take it; and a second, nocturnal life, the legacy of shimmers and shadows, of fugitive moments, of scenes half-lived half-dreamed: the life of a woman who is now taking her leave.

Alice was born to be a queen; then fate made a mistake. Her luminous eyes, her angelic smile would have given heart to a whole downcast nation. Her soft broad shoulders, straight and proud, were made to display, heedless of their weight, ermine, velvet, and millennial gems, and the smoothness of her brow to be caressed by strands of dangling, milky pearls.

In accounts of her childhood and dreary youth, everything recalled the sad beginnings of tales whose raggedy heroine ends up a princess. Year after year, I waited for this miracle that never happened. Why had no fairy alleviated her ordeals and set a crown on her head instead of gray hairs? I used to think there was no limit to her patience. How could she preserve such a smile and such confidence?

In a desk drawer she kept a box of which she was particularly fond. It contained an assortment of snapshots, letters, old postcards, sky-blue pendants of the Virgin Mary, mother-of-pearl buttons, foreign coins. The gilt box was octagonal, with a surface that felt uneven to the touch, overlaid as it was with a fine lacy relief of dull gold. At the center of the lid was an oval medallion that reproduced in pastel colors the delicate smiling face of Queen Astrid. The sight of this portrait left me spellbound—the two women were so alike, it might have been her own.

Astrid of Belgium was young, beautiful, and much loved. She would, more or less, be your age. A small, finely chased diadem brightened the undulations of her hair; her white neck emerged from an impeccable fur collar. Her death was a "tragic" one, wept over by every newspaper in Europe: a car accident that orphaned two children and left a king in despair. In the depths of the box, clipped from a magazine article, were photographs of the royal family and, next to them, the shattered car.

Alice used to tell the melancholy tale of Astrid, whom she loved like a sister and who, she said, deserved a kinder fate. As I listened to her I could sense how she identified herself with the dead queen, whose memory was laden with her own regrets and all the sorrows still ahead of her. It was as if the only thing that could resemble her was an image of suffering; as if, to her life, only a life steeped in doom could be declared a parallel.

Es war einmal . . . Once upon a time, though, when she was seventeen, everything had been like a fairy tale.

She was a well-behaved, timid adolescent who lived with her sister, three years her elder, and their widowed mother. In Mulhouse, the twenties for them weren't exactly roaring. The vagaries of Paris fashion had grown fairly tame before reaching their part of the country, where, under the stern eyes of mother and grandmothers who would have felt jeopardized in the eyes of God and men if they revealed one inch of ankle, youth was anything but daring. Girls were pointed at and called sluts when they started hemming their skirts at the knee to make dancing the Charleston easier, or chopped off their turn-of-the-century braids for the sake of a trimmer, boyish look.

In Mulhouse (Haut-Rhin Department), distractions were few. The two sisters were devotees of the dancing school—the one place where meeting boys was tolerated, where trying out an adventurous new dress was permissible, and where what was essential was learning the steps that would enable them to catch a beau (perhaps even a husband) on the ballroom floor at some official dance in the small town.

Since her widowhood, their mother had been struggling against poverty and a heart condition to ensure a decent sustenance for her children, as well as an upbringing suitable for "eligible young ladies." Life would have been less harsh if Anna hadn't fallen out with her own mother: at the war's end she had fled her devastating authority. "I'd rather be poor on my own than dependent on a wealthy harpy," she used to say with a laugh. The two sisters had no dowry; but their trousseau was ready. They were accomplished in sewing, embroidery, and playing the piano—in other words, they had what it took to become engaged. Some day, perhaps, luck would arrange a meeting with a respectable man—a merchant with property of his own, or a well-to-do young widower. Alice secretly prayed that fate would not force her into a "good match" that would reassure her mother about her future. She wanted love, nothing but passionate love, and while she embroidered her nightgowns, she was waiting for Prince Charming.

Her sister was the first to find a husband. The winter they married, Alice was seventeen and feverishly preparing for her first ball, at the Mulhouse College of Chemical Engineering. Too ill to play her role as chaperone, Anna delegated the task to her eldest daughter, now "settled." The evening was a source of some anxiety to her in prospect. The young chemists, who were very rowdy, frequently made the town buzz with their practical jokes. No one had forgotten the morning when the main street had woken to an appalling racket—its garbage cans had all been strung together on a rope tied to the back of a garbage truck making its rounds; or the day when frightened pedestrians found a crocodile swimming in the ornamental pool on the main square. A zealous policeman had actually fired a shot at it. This produced a notably metallic ring, and no wonder: the monster was actually the sign of a restaurant called The Crocodile and had been taken down by those college scamps during the night.

A thousand times over Anne advised Alice to be careful and well-behaved—if your grandmother knew you were in such a sinful place she'd pop her corset! Alice promised to be good.

Before the big day, her mother insisted that she be photographed in her pretty mauve dress, whose collar and low waist she had adorned with a pattern of stiff muslin pansies. Alice always kept this portrait: it was a souvenir of the most wonderful day in her life. In it she looks like the romantic woman of one's dreams against the background of *trompe-l'oeil* clouds, standing erect, her head bent as if swaying in the breeze that quickens the cardboard sky, while her hand rests nonchalantly on a gilt wood credenza.

Who could number the times she has sat in reverie in front of that oval picture frame? The ball might have turned out quite differently that night, and then she would never have dreamed her life away with him. It makes her head spin reliving that moment when, in the flash of their meeting, everything was settled. She might still have brushed against his back, jostled his elbow in the crush, blushed after spilling his drink and knocking cigarette ash over the jacket of his impeccable young officer's uniform—and then forgotten him and rushed onto the dance floor on someone else's arm. Or he might have ignored her awkwardness and gone on talking man's talk, or perhaps for the next tango invited the blonde, or the young lady in blue flounces, or the excited girl in pink who was laughing so loud. But no: that night he was the hero and she was the heroine of a novel that time was writing for them. No sooner had their eyes met in fleeting appeal than that decisive moment already was part of their past.

In my darkness, I can see the young girl in mauve in the middle of the crowd. I can imagine her emotion and the faint giddiness that transports her as she goes into the ballroom and breathes in the first sounds of dancing. That night she may not have been the gayest woman, or the most confident; but beneath the crystal chandeliers of the vast, austere hall, rimmed with dark paneling and leatherette settees, in the midst of the laughter, the waltzing, and the petticoats, she was the only one he saw.

He was chatting at the bar with a group of young men, no doubt discussing politics, careers, the future. Soon they would start talking about the young ladies, making enthusiastic or ironic remarks about their dresses and hairdos. Each would then choose one of the lovelies and, with a becoming bow, invite her to join in the dancing.

But then she makes her entry and, as in a movie, all eyes turn toward her. As for him, I can see him leave his drink on the bar; someone whispers in his ear, takes him by the arm, and leads him to her. He tells the others, "I'll be back." But he won't be back.

As a joke, the band is playing an old-fashioned quadrille. The floor trembles, bits of color are bobbing up and down among laughing faces. Along the walls, the mothers' hats straighten up, eyes stare anxiously at the middle of the room. Can you dance *that* in a short skirt?

They are introduced. Alice distractedly proffers her hand. From her wrist a velvet reticule dangles on a gilded chain. She doesn't catch his name; he sees nothing but her eyes. Side by side they watch the dancers' merry-go-round. Enchanted by the spectacle, she has clasped her hands under her uplifted chin. He is entirely preoccupied by the mauve dress, the garland of pansies encircling the white neck, the pink cheeks and black lashes, the reticule brushing against her bosom at the end of its chain.

Then, without knowing how—applause has acknowledged the end of the square dance, the band has barely started "The Blue

Danube"—she is in his arms. All that separates their faces are her chestnut locks and the scent of the lavender water with which he must have doused himself.

He danced badly, but all night long. The waxed floor squeaked in places; near the bar it had lost its polish from spilt white wine. All night long her brown moiré pumps followed in the steps (a trifle awkward at first, more confident by dawn) of his patent leather shoes.

Alice's sister has to wait a long, long time. Through sleeping streets she brings Alice home on her cloud. Streetlamps are extinguished in the morning fog. Going up the stairs, they keep laughing all the way to the apartment door, which Anna soundlessly opens, revealing to the early morning an insomniac's face and a voice stifled with anxiety.

"Good Lord, what have you been doing so late?"

Enfolding her in her soft arms, Alice, drunk with sleep, tells her that she is engaged. By the time her mother faints she is already sound asleep on the couch in the hall, amid the crumpled folds of her mauve dress, hugging the velvet reticule to her heart.

The night wore on. I keep expecting to hear something stirring; but it's the hour between night and morning when, even in Paris, everything is calm. There is only from time to time the distant growl of a car; and, much nearer, the throbbing tick tock of the alarm clock that fills my head. It's the hour when the sleep of city dwellers is deep, before the familiar noises of morning. Juliette has fallen asleep. I'm sitting alone, facing the empty chair. Soon I'll hear the wine merchant rolling up his iron curtain, the clash of bottles in wooden crates, the metallic sound of stands being set up on the sidewalk. Today is market day.

But for the moment it's still the damp bitter time when the eyelids of those standing watch grow heavy, the time when night owls are returning from their festivities, the time when you came home from the ball. If I had moved out of the red circle of the little lamp that insulates me from this baneful night, if I groped my way to your room, perhaps the door would open on a seventeen-year-old young woman, asleep in a mauve dress sprigged with faded pansies: perhaps, perhaps . . . if the stories you once told me were not tall tales, and if the years, the wearing years, hadn't killed Sleeping Beauty.

I sit rooted to my chair. Morning is tracing gray stripes on the blind, and I wish I could utterly expel from my weariness the image of an old woman I no longer know, now lying in the depths of a most incomprehensible solitude. Around me objects are emerging from the shadows. It's as though they were speaking of you through a veil—as if, no longer destined to exist in the light of your gaze, your touch, your scent, they were withdrawing from the oncoming day that will render them forever useless; as if they were already vanishing into the museum of oblivion.

I almost fell asleep. Rousing myself, anxious not to sink into some cloying dream—boarded up in a wooden tunnel, or suffocating under monstrous quilts—I get up and walk over to the row of photographs above the piano. Among the glassed-in images that now reflect the faint light of day filtering in from outside, I rediscover the young woman standing next to her fiancé, looking very serious. His parents insisted on the photograph; she could have done without it. She didn't have the heart to pose among baskets of carnations and hydrangeas, and asked for a plain backdrop. Her dress is dark-colored and belted at the hips. Not a single jewel. Her hair is cut short; her gaze is infinitely remote. He stands very straight, his face emerging sharply from the collar of his uniform, in which he seems a little stiff, with his gloved hands clasped in front of him. They don't look like a couple. And yet they adore each other.

Alice's mother had been getting worse and worse, and the engagement would have been announced under rather gloomy circumstances had not the fiancé's parents arrived, bringing with them in their shiny limousine all the glamor of Parisian chic. The cases of champagne that the future father-in-law solemnly unloaded made a strong impression on Alice's grandmother, who had made peace with her daughter for the occasion. Behind her pince-nez, her contented glance shifted from the fiancé's mother's silver foxes to his father's elegant fur-lined overcoat, taking in on the way, among other things, the pearl necklace, diamond earrings, and the gold watch chain.

Once the ball was over, bringing matters to this point hadn't been simple. "She's much too young." "He hasn't finished college." "He's a chemical engineer," Anna complained, thinking of the crocodile. "He's a nice enough looking young man," Grandmother declared, "but he has no moustache, my dear, and that is not proper."—"You had to choose a foreigner for your wife," his father grumbled—he was a decorated veteran of World War I for whom Alsace was still part of Germany and who—most important—had picked out for his son a plump heiress from his own neck of the woods. "You shouldn't have sent me to Mulhouse," the son retorted. "I've lost my heart—I won't settle for anyone but her." As for Alice, she threatened to jump off the roof of the Strasbourg cathedral . . . And so they were engaged.

The marriage took place, amid tears, two years later. Anna never saw her daughter in white: a final attack carried her off several weeks before the event. On their wedding night, after a walk through the cemetery, where a trembling Alice laid her tulle-wrapped bridal bouquet on her mother's grave, they left Alsace for good.

1924. Forty years of age between the two of them. With his engineer's diploma in his pocket, he has a brilliant future ahead of him; at nineteen she is an orphan, but married. Her heart is divided between love and mourning. She has abandoned her childhood on a white stone; but her bouquet of everlastings will not fade, any more than her past years, which she would like to swallow down forever, along with her grief, so as to resonate simply and hopefully to the new music of their life together.

My eyelids are burning. It's getting lighter and lighter in the room. I look at the wedding pictures and stretch out my hand toward the melancholy bride: the glass lies cold over the lovely face, hemmed with tulle and little white roses. A rustle of cloth startles me. No, she hasn't sat down in her chair, buried in her lace ruching. It's time to wake up. Still out of sight, the morning sun is hurting my eyes, concentrating its pale blaze on the white wall of the building at the back of the yard. The blinds are being pulled up; the warm fragrance of toast invades the room. Juliette sets a tray in front of me.

"You didn't sleep?"

"I think I did."

"Did you take a look at her?"

"Yes. Actually, I didn't."

"She hasn't budged. That's no normal sleep. You better make up your mind. Drink your coffee and get on the phone."

I'll get on the phone. But they won't tell me anything new about her. I know everything, and I've had enough. I'll say, "She's sleeping," and I'll hear, "That's not normal. Well, well, we'd better come and take a look." They'll arrive with knowledge, cold equipment, and a serious manner. They'll lift up the sheet; I can't prevent that. They will observe that she's soaked. She can no longer "help" herself—another revealing symptom. They will raise first one leg, then the other: no reaction. And they will say, nodding their heads, "There's no possible doubt. Sound asleep. Just as we expected." The right side of her brain, which controlled the left side of her body, has been in turn overwhelmed. The dam has burst; the borrowed time has run out; it's all over. She used to sit up; now she's flat on her back. I've had enough.

If we were far away from cities, noise, and the civilized world—if we were on a shore where only sun and wind, forest and storm could dispose of our lives, I wouldn't phone. I'd walk barefoot through sand to a hut made of branches, and there I would set up a shrine. I would erect a bed of palm fronds and flowers and lay her down on it. When the sun set, there would be many outside chanting as they waited for her last breath to be exhaled and for her soul to fly up among the stars. But we're in Paris between concrete walls, chimney pots block the sky, and we no longer know how to die. We no longer know the rites. We no longer dare face death because nothing holy or beautiful now prepares us for it. When it approaches, we run away. We conceal it in hospitals, those gaping wounds, those meeting places of solitude and oblivion.

If we were far away from cities—very far away—I would simply watch you sleep, accompanying you without regret until your sleep had run its course. But you can't keep a ghost at home. Hospitals were built for a purpose. They'll palpate, auscultate, and shake you. Where there's life . . . And take you away. Enough.

For me she's already left. Take her body, it's all yours. Sleep protects her like an embalmed mummy's wrappings. Yes, I'll get on the phone. You'll hear me speaking reasonably, describing a clinical case that is easy to identify. You'll come to verify what I told you, and you'll see me acquiesce when you pronounce the inevitable diagnosis. You'll see how very calmly I follow the ambulance to the hospital of your choice, how quietly I sit at the head of the sleeping woman's bed, alert to the development of a medical phenomenon affecting this body that has been confided to your care. You won't see or hear anything else. But now that silence has flooded her eyes and her voice, I'll remain with a woman you've never known, and speak to her living face of earlier times.

Before you carry her helplessly away, I'll remove the necklace of memories from her neck, unhook the little glazed shrines, and catalogue their relics; I'll decipher them and tell their stories, then smash the lids of the glass jars. Memories will fly their coop, and I shall inscribe them in the sky, every last one of them. While you are becoming keepers of her body and putting her death throes under surveillance, as if determined to intercept a message that was never meant for you, I for my part will take charge of her life.

I want to discover that woman of former days, the one revealed as she leafed through albums and diaries, the one preserved under glass on the walls of her prison. I don't want either to absolve or prettify her; I want to cry out to her, across the void that is widening between us, that she can depart in all tranquility and bequeath her life to me. I won't mount it in a frame, since I have no home of my own to hang memories in. I won't tie it up in ribbons or let it yellow among my love letters in some desk drawer—my life will never be cluttered with such furniture. All I want is to travel through her life like a migrating bird, looking down on its shores, seas, and lagoons, its forests and mountains, alighting wherever she's left her imprint, retracing her path by following the marks she has inscribed or erased, pausing by the signs she has strewn across the years, whether they be white stones or black.

I want to lie down in her cradle, put on her petticoats, lace up her ankle boots. I want to learn how to read from her books. I want to cross the gray cobblestones of Mulhouse holding her mother's hand. I want to embroider her trousseau, pricking my finger in the oil lamp's circle of light, and sit at her piano playing four-hand pieces by Mozart. I want to attend that ball and vibrate to the caress of a first waltz. I want to leave Alsace and feel my first child budding in my womb. I want to wait up for the man she loves, open my arms to him, and see him leave once again. Again waiting for him and forgiving him and resenting him, too, for always moving on. I want to sing through the night and pace the floors of a house asleep amid dank autumn gardens. Silently compose the monotony of her days and keep quiet with her and weep because nothing once lived through can be altered. But I would also like to understand why I keep quiet and weep and go on loving and sacrificing myself and so stubbornly play the role of obedient wife. I want to keep going, adjuring heaven, rushing all day long around town, tiring out my body, telling my child as I rock him to sleep that his father is a hero. One day see the hero return from his crusades (scarcely any calmer, and ready to devour new life like a cannibal); after that, no longer able to play the wife, collapse; and at the end, quite gently, quite simply, grow old with her on her bed of ashes and pass away.

The ambulance has had to double-park between the meat-and-tripe butcher and the mechanized lacemaker (handkerchiefs five for ten francs). Two rows of trucks overflowing with crates and cartons are drawn up along sidewalks that are jammed with Friday's outdoor market. It's a luminous October morning. The street is shimmering in a coolness whose veil the sun will shortly lift, and resounding with the first shouts of the vendors and the clatter of unfolding stalls. The air smells of fresh fish, leeks, greens.

The bus draws to a stop behind the ambulance: six inches too few. A line of cars accumulates, unable to see what's happening, and a din of horns fills the street with a thick layer of sound that floats up to the rooftops and unravels among television antennas. The bus driver gets out, goes to the back of his vehicle, and, turning toward the cars, raises his arms in an expression of helplessness and reproach. Heads are turned, arms are waving, indignation is brewing among the pedestrians. Beret askew, a little old pensioner threatens the motley, stinking, snorting snake with his cane. There's a flurry of dishtowels, brooms, and heads in windows. Eyes bulge, forefingers are screwed against temples—what's wrong with you, can't you see it's an ambulance?

I'm standing stiffly, rooted to the doormat, my forehead glued to the pane of the street door. I'm a statue of imitation marble that is taking on the "modern" gray-blue-white speckling of the doorframe. My motionless image hangs impersonally suspended in the play of the lobby mirrors. I look at a swarming street, the white elongated shape of an ambulance beyond salads, tomatoes, and Spanish oranges. Inside I'm shivering with panic. The two stretcher-bearers are panting and swearing in the stairway, whose corners "carrying this thing" makes so hard to manage. "How do they build these dumps—they sure don't think about sick people. Shit, what a job!" The stretcher bangs against wall and railing. With each thud or metallic clang something falls from my throat into the pit of my stomach, then floats back up. My eyelids shut. In elevators do they stand coffins on their ends?

The men in white arrive, sweating hard. "She's certainly no lightweight. What a life! Well, we made it." The inner door squeaks as it swings heavily against the stretcher with a faint sound. "Watch out for her hand," one of them says. "No reaction—she doesn't feel a thing." My forehead and boots free themselves laboriously from pane and doormat. I watch her being bumpily trundled past. She's asleep. Misty white locks still curl around the white face turned on one side. A trickle of saliva drips from her parted lips onto the handkerchief I've slipped beneath her cheek.

It's too late to send the ambulance back, return to the living room's dusty silence, and sit her down in her chair once again. No way to turn back. People are all around us shouting, staring, living their lives. I hate them for the racket, for the colors, for their gaiety. Loveless curious eyes will settle their gaze on her brow. Irreverent faces will turn and indifferently follow our ridiculous passage through the chicories and pippins.

How I miss you! How I suddenly wish you could see us making our way between the vegetables! Would you burst out in that abrupt throaty laugh I loved so much, the way you sometimes did in moments of unbearable tension? Would you laugh at my gloomy expression half-hidden, thank God, behind tinted glasses? Would you laugh at the sweaty, congested faces of your two nurses and the grim looks of the onlookers? Or would you complain bitterly that I had turned you helplessly loose in the crowd, that I was letting you be carried by nameless strangers, inadequately wrapped up in a rough blanket—you so fastidious—without having even combed your hair or powdered your nose?

I'll never forget the insipid smell of raw meat that accompanied your last outing, mingled with the glorious one of leeks in sunlight.

The inhuman transfers that cities impose on us, the streets of cities, the life of cities—our siren shrieks as we pass through neighborhoods, some of them bustling, others empty, all with life in them somewhere, heads screwed around, red lights run, corners taken on two wheels, streets stretching ahead as far as the wall marked HOSPITAL.

. . . I remember, she used to say, the cherry trees were in blossom. It was one of those beautiful, luminous springs that sometimes burst forth in Alsace after an icy winter. We were allowed to play outside. Often we'd look up at the sky, on alert for bird cries and beating wings. We were waiting for the storks to return. There was a nest perched on the church steeple. As soon as a flock of birds appeared on the horizon, high above the fields flecked with pink and white petals, all the children in the village would gather in the church square. They would wave their arms and shout excitedly to summon the graceful creatures wheeling about the steeple, clacking their beaks and spreading their broad, black-edged, gently swaying wings. On the day when one touched down on the nest to settle there at the end of her journey, perhaps calling its mate with a few clattering yet tender cries, the jubilant children would join hands in a wild round dance.

I was five at the time. I can still smell the fresh scent of blue air and the first hyacinths in the gardens—tiny, impeccable, neatly laid out—that fronted each house on the square. As soon as our father fell ill, we had left Mulhouse and moved to the country, where we lived in a postcard village that curled around a pointed steeple and was surrounded as far as the eye could see with fields of hops and meadows planted with fruit trees.

It must have been a Saturday. We were running alongside wagons that were on their way to market. My mother appeared in the distance. She was walking smoothly toward us; her long gray cotton dress, under a bright white starched apron, swung as she went. Smiling, she beckoned to us. On her arm hung a vast basket covered with a red-and-white checked dishtowel. Our father was waiting for us in the cart, behind our old donkey, who had been decked out in a bonnet of faded blue denim. "Let's go," she said to my sister and me, "we're having a picnic."

All four of us went singing, I remember, down a little acacia-bordered path. My father picked a spot in the meadows where buttercups spangled thick clover that exhaled its fragrance in the noonday sun. He spread a blanket underneath a thickset cherry tree whose branches, overladen with blossoms, would now and then release clouds of pearl-white petals to the breeze that had set them quivering. My father was very tall; he seemed positively huge to me against the sky, in a full-sleeved shirt caught at the waist by a red-flannel waistband. His teeth glistened beneath his black mustache. I can still recall his male smell as it mingled with the raw fragrance of the grass. He plucked off my straw hat and with a laugh sent it flying; then, pulling me against him by my pigtails, he spilled us both onto the sloping clover. He'd been drinking white wine and couldn't stop laughing. We careened downhill until we reached the hat. I was gasping for joy, my face was buried against his warm neck.

I'm not too sure what happened next. My mother's anxious face was peering down at us. My father was coughing, flat on his back, his eyes shut as he fanned his sweaty forehead with my hat. We had to go home then and there. Mother took the reins. I was sad I hadn't had time to make a bouquet. There was no more singing. Father, very pale, held a handkerchief tight against his mouth.

To reach our house we had to cross the square in front of the church. Children were waving their handkerchiefs skyward and dancing for joy. A stork and her young one had chosen to settle on the belfry. Spreading wide their wings, they seemed to be acknowledging the noisy tribute with perfect dignity.

My father was confined to his room. He refused to go back to a sanatorium in Switzerland: he didn't want to leave us. Several months later—it was Christmas Eve, I remember—we were singing around the lighted Christmas tree. Father got up, in his long velvet bathrobe, took my hand and then my sister's, and led us in a dance around the tree. The candle flames flickered and cast their wavering light on our faces. I can still hear my mother's scream. He'd fallen suddenly, his ankles twisting, caught in the folds of his robe, and he lay unconscious on the rug, his face contracted and very pale, scarcely tinged by the candlelight.

Later that night a carriage drew up to our door. Two men in dark suits brought out a stretcher. I was very cold; I remember their frosty breath and bent backs, how they rubbed their hands together and complained about being called out on a night like this. They laid my father on the stretcher. We bent down to kiss him; his cheeks were moist. He told us to be good, then disappeared into the night, accompanied by snow and the horses' white breath . . .

If you shop on the Rue Saint-Charles with the eleven-o'clock crowd, you have a hard time making your way between the outdoor stands of the shops and those of the stallholders, all laden with mountains of fresh food. They're being awfully rash with their stretcher. They'll have to pass between a hillock of lettuce and pyramids of eggs. What else can they do? As I hold the door open for our unusual procession, I'm threatened with a painful attack of giggles: I see the dumbfounded face of the grocer's wife—her "Salad at a good price!" sticks in her vocal cords. We plunge with dignity between two lines of shopping bags, amid appropriate murmurings, as far as the open doors of the ambulance. To distract myself, I imagine her amusement: "More fun on a sunny market day, isn't it? But you might have put out more flowers, and less fish."

With a roar the ambulance carries us away. The bus can start moving, the cars can stop honking, the grocer's wife can sell her vegetables and the street carry on its noisy life without us. As if nothing had happened. As if you were still waiting in your armchair for Juliette to come back and empty the contents of the shopping basket in front of you.

Before we pass through the hospital entrance, a few minutes remain for wishful thinking, for believing all this is not real. Soon an atmosphere of plaster, hypodermics, and ether will envelop your motionless body and your willful silence. Go on, complain! Start screaming! Stick up for yourself! Don't let them lock you up in their white prison. One word from you and we could leave the Boulevard Périphérique and take the thruway south. One laugh from you and we could stop at Orly and take a flight wherever you like. But you won't do it. You've given up.

Behind those sealed eyes, she's no longer calling for me. Three beads of sweat trickle across her hollowed temple. Her head bounces to and fro at each jolt of the pavement. No expression disturbs her face, as smooth as still water, and as cold.

We're expected at Dr. X's intensive care unit. It's located in a separate, ultra-modern construction at the far end of the main driveway, beyond the grayish or yellowing blocks of more dilapidated buildings. The place is anything but squalid. There are trees, and benches on which, in sunlight, a number of scattered pajama-clad shapes are rediscovering reality. There are beds of dahlias and dwarf chrysanthemums.

"You're in luck—they're letting her in," is what our doctor had told me this morning, with a hint of triumph in his voice as he hung up. After a detailed and eloquent presentation that had gratified him with success, he had just had her accepted by Dr. Z, an exceptionally competent colleague of his. "No easy matter, you know, in her condition. But he's interested in the case because she's young." I had warmly thanked him and then ventured, "Otherwise?" "Otherwise? Oh—" with, presumably, a vague wave of his hand and an emphatic nod, "otherwise, it's no picnic. Routine care, a ward for bedridden cases. And who knows where? Wherever they'd take her." "So you see we've been spared the worst," Juliette reassured me, cutting short a potentially disastrous conversation.

The echoing tiled corridor smells of formalin and bleach. A most amiable intern is on hand to receive us. The ambulance men have hurriedly deposited their burden on a gurney. A room has yet to be allocated. They have me sign a piece of paper, then wait, looking at me . . . In a panic I start rummaging in my handbag and extract a crumpled bill, which I then hand to them. (My inevitable uneasiness and exasperating shyness whenever there's a tip to be given.)

"Madame, hello there!" the intern is shouting. I turn around. Bending over her, he vigorously shakes her by one shoulder, then the other. "Hello there!" Displeased by the lack of response, he sharply lifts the head and drops it; after which, with the blanket turned down, I actually see him take her nipples between his fingers and pinch them, then straighten up, perplexed. I want to scream and hit him, but I'm paralyzed with horror. I'm incapable of raising my hand and slapping him when, very sure of himself, he says to me threateningly, "We're going to wake her up, you can bet on that!" But what will they do to her to wake her up? At the back of my head a voice is droning: Keep calm, keep calm, this is what goes on in hospitals, he's only an intern, not a butcher . . . My cheeks stiffen, my teeth clench. I can barely mutter, "Please, don't hurt her."

And here he is, solicitously taking me by the arm and leading me away down the corridor. My mind's in turmoil—they're going to administer sedation and lock me up. Get out, get out. But the benevolent intern keeps humoring me; and, pathetically, I collapse in tears on a chair set against a glossy wall. I, too, have given up.

I'm abandoning her. She's in their hands. She belongs to them. They will do "everything they can to save her"—to bring her back to life. What do they know of her life? By what right do they intend to bring her back to it? We are all now caught up in the mechanism of gradual death. We are passive agents in the useless struggle that will play itself out between four white walls, where "no trouble will be spared" to try and delay an outcome already inscribed in the stars or on the brow or in the palm of the hand. There is an unknown date that follows us like a shadow from the morning to the evening of life, as indelibly inscribed on us as a tattoo: the moment when everything comes to a stop. Why are we so afraid of that moment when at last we sense that it's here, right next to us, just beyond the bedroom door? Why do we erect against it this tentacular human apparatus of impossible rescue that is bound to break down on the appointed day, at the appointed hour?

What I wanted for you was peace amid flowers and silk, with a Bach cantata in the background; not this iron bed, stiff sheets, bellowing voices indifferent to your rest: not this snare. Go on sleeping. Don't open your eyes on this methodical nightmare. Don't come back yet, if you must come back: you would see that I'd betrayed you.

They've tucked her quite properly and snugly into the clean bed by a window overlooking the parking lot, in a double room whose second bed is empty. I hurriedly turn off the radiator (the heat is stifling), fling open the window, and quickly lower the blinds. Seeing her face asleep in blazing sunlight is unbearable.

A well-mannered, tidy-looking nurse tiptoes in and walks around the bed—not doing anything, just taking a look. She has no orders yet concerning treatment. Dr. Z will stop by this afternoon. We smile at each other. She goes out but leaves the door ajar—turning round, she asks me though the aperture in a faint, very cheery voice, "Has she been in a coma long?"

It's the first time I've heard the word. It breaks over me like a wave of muddy water or a fog of brownish rough wool. Coma . . . ah . . . ahhhh . . . Falling down a well, circles in the water . . . Deep coma; sleep beyond reach; halfway to death. There's a question I have to answer:

"Yes, a long time. Well, I'm not sure anymore. Everything was going fine. She was sitting in her chair. She was bored with the program on TV. She was knitting, the cat was asleep on the table, and then . . ." (The little lady is patiently listening. Whatever am I talking about?) "Tell me something: do people ever wake up from this sort of coma?"

"Why, of course. We'll take care of her. She's young. Her heart is perfectly sound."

"Oh, the heart's all right . . . It's her head. You can't listen to her head. You can't know what's happening inside her head."

"We'll find out, don't you worry. We'll find out. We're fully equipped."

She clearly finds me entertaining. Off she goes.

. . . I remember, you used to say, it was cold, it was mid December. We drove the whole night without stopping. Grandmother had given me a basket, with cinnamon cookies and two thermoses of coffee. "Why don't you wait till tomorrow," she had said as she helped me shut my trunk, where there was no room for my bridal gown. "*Kinder*, in cold like this, are you going to sleep in the snow, *oder was*?" Her bracelets tinkled. "And I haven't given you my advice, *ach*, I hope your mother told you about marriage, at least a little."

I gave her a kiss to shut her up. It must have been while I was standing in front of the lobby mirror putting on my coat that she hid the two gingerbread Santa Clauses in the bottom of the basket, under a dishcloth. Of course I broke down when I found them. We laughed happily as we ate them—our last morsels of Alsace.

In the small hours we arrived at the engineer's cottage that had been readied for us. Nearby, the factory emerged from the foggy darkness in its wreath of night lights, fitfully spattered with glittering gusts from its huge, perpetually flaming smokestack. In the yellow glare of our headlights the house came into view, surrounded by hoarfrost, looking with its fresh stucco and bolted shutters as if it had given up waiting for us. But the key had been left under the first overturned flowerpot. Three steps led up to the door. Switching on the current was an achievement of heroic proportions. Unfortunately, no one had remembered to screw bulbs into the sockets dangling sadly from the ceilings. Walls of still-damp plaster wrapped us in icy air. Our flashlight led us to the flower-papered bedroom. Some kind soul had kindled a fire the day before (and left us a bucket of coal by the stove), and a thick red quilt had been spread on the bed.

Our wedding night began at daybreak: a strange frosty night punctuated with smoke from a stove that didn't draw, hot-water bottles, flannel nightshirts torn off by hands that trembled (with cold), gooseflesh, giggles, hot toddies spilled on the pillows—certainly the merriest night of my life.

Nine months later to the day, I gave birth to my first child, a son. We were happy then, truly happy. Naturally I felt a little out of place, a little lonely in that part of the world. But he'd bring his friends home for the evening and we'd listen to music, or I'd play the piano and, if I knew them really well, sometimes I'd sing. A second son was born not long after. As a mother, I was completely happy; as a wife, I was, without a doubt, both loved and wildly loving. The sweetest years of my life were spent there, in an ugly little industrial town and an unattractive cottage, among my children, the geraniums on my windowsill, and the well-mannered wives of other engineers whom I used to meet for tea and rummy; and with a man at my side who was then full of consideration, who never forgot my birthday, who used to bury me in flowers on the slightest pretext. I may not have been very demanding, but that modest life delighted me.

He, I could feel, was starting to champ at the bit. His work was very much appreciated, but he could never get enough of it, never be satisfied with his responsibilities. Was it ambition that made him want to conquer the world? I don't think so. He was certainly proud—he never stopped challenging himself. Tireless by nature, he wanted action, action, more action. And I tagged along, with no premonition of the whirlwind into which he was drawing us.

There were two or three luminous summers on a Mediterranean shore. I'd never seen the sea before; I was entranced. Mimosas, cicadas, the smell of pines, the red earth of Esterel, the sun, the hinterland all hills and olive groves—pure enchantment. Those years—the thirties—were the sweetest of my life . . .

Memories! She had fought for memories her whole life: not letting anything slip by, holding time back, taming its flow, consecrating it through sacred rites of remembrance. Weaving garlands out of insignificant details, ordinary events, and trivial reactions so as later to discover, at the moment when it was least expected, a voice's warmth, an evening's hue, a caress, or the pain of a farewell.

As a little girl she had loved making assemblages of delicate dried plants or butterfly wings. She loved catching and keeping something of the creatures crossing her path that would serve as a means of recalling them later.

As soon as she was old enough to write, she started using her fine regular script to fill up the ruled pages of notebooks of various sizes, all bound in cloth and decorated with naïve drawings. There, noting the date, she would set down her smallest thoughts, or copy out poems and sayings.

She sometimes allowed me to thumb through these yellow-edged notebooks, their corner frayed from being opened so often, to be written in or reread. Some pages displayed fine pencil drawings of bouquets, beribboned hampers, children's faces. These illustrations had been dated and signed by a variety of hands: "A souvenir of Emilie" or "On this beautiful summer day, your dear friend, Gertrude." There were sentences in French or German, depending on the friend and the year, some in mysterious Gothic script. In places the pages bulged with pressed flowers once glued in place, bits of which now stuck in the gutters between pages, others having vanished into dust when the fragile thing had been too roughly handled. She kept these precious relics the way she kept everything—report cards, diplomas, the holy images from her confirmation, letters, her father's watch: everything that connected her with the emotions of her childhood past. Returning to this dusty museum reassured her. It gave her a sense of the continuity of her feelings; it was a justification of her fate.

Her childhood memories were those that she apparently valued most. It was as if behind the profusion of her brown hair and limpid eyes the little girl of 1914, the child of the Great War, held all the secrets of the woman she was to become. Alsace was her paradise lost, the fondly remembered land that held the roots she had one day severed to go off with the man of her life.

It is said that when age starts verging on old age, it disturbs the workings of the memory and makes it more selective: distant images reappear clearly, whereas the more immediate past tends to fade into the twilight zone that often follows maturity and ushers in an age that is called ripe precisely because the ripening process has ended. She wasn't old as yet; but by upsetting the functioning of her mind, infirmity had hastened the process of an unconscious rediscovery of her childhood.

Among all the characters that had marked her life and become the heroes of her personal saga, it was still the little heroine in the black stockings and white petticoats whom she loved best. It was for this Alice from a lost wonderland that she reacquired her old fondness for ruled notebooks in cloth bindings. She picked one covered in mauve and undertook a fragmented reconstruction of particular childhood memories. The writing was uneven and awkward, full of ups and downs, full of interruptions in mid-word, broken with sighs and complaints about her clumsiness. Her left hand—after her attack, she had trained it to hold a pencil—didn't always respond to the tugs of recollection. Among those pages (there are few of them, because soon she was unable to write at all, her final months being spent in a state of giddiness that set everything swimming before her eyes) I rediscovered, one day when I happened to be putting things away, the little girl about whom she had so often spoken.

. . . At school the other children would never take me by the hand. I could never play with them in a ring: I always hid my left hand in the pocket my mother added to all my clothes. I had been born with six fingers on that hand. It had an extra thumb, for no particular reason—our family was quite 'untainted.' My grandmother had shouted over my cradle, 'The child is a freak!' It took my gentle mother a while to get over that. I was operated on when I was a few months old, but the surgeon got the thumbs mixed up and removed the good one. Afterwards there were more operations, since the good thumb, no doubt taking its revenge, insisted on reasserting itself as a bony protuberance. I was ashamed of my deformity; it was what kept other children at a distance. At the age of ten my hand looked normal enough, but the thumb remained weak: it was smaller, atrophied, and stiffer than the other one. It did not prevent me from playing the piano, but it did, to my despair, bar the way to becoming the concert performer I later dreamed of being.

Grandmother was a very fine pianist. She said that as a young woman she had charmed many a provincial drawing room but that subsequently she had never had a chance to broaden her audience. She became a teacher and trained a great many students with whom she was infinitely less strict than she was with me. During lessons, she would stand next to the plum-colored velvet stool on which I was perched like a feather ready to be flown away at the first gust of her frequent temper tantrums. Looking most impressive in her full black skirt, she would keep nervously twisting a ruler in her mitt-covered hands, adjust her pince-nez as she bent over the score, or tap on the toe of one high-button shoe in time with the ticking metronome. Sitting on the piano and staring at me out of china-blue eyes, Blanc-blanc—Grandmother's stuffed cat—frightened me no less than she did.

My childhood memories are precise moments of pain. I already had a marked inclination for suffering.

I lost my father when I was six—a vast sorrow whose reverberations I still feel. Winter nights when anguish would start with the candle lighted at the bottom of the creaking stairs, continuing in the cold bedroom with its shadowy walls and an over-starched cotton nightgown that was too big for me, brought to its peak between the sheets where I lay with my feet cold and my eyelids shut tight: waiting for his good night kiss weeping because I would never again sniff the spicy fragrance of his skin or the smell of Virginia tobacco on his mustache. "He'll never come back, he's in heaven." I thought we were going to walk right up to heaven the day Grandmother solemnly told us, "We are taking him to his final resting place." I can still see the pathetic little procession in the streets of Mulhouse, led by two children hidden beneath black veils. My mother hung on Grandfather's arm, crying. It was a warm day.

I adored my grandfather. He alone was strong and kept watch over my wary existence. He did his best to replace my young father, the thought of whom often left me downcast. I never spoke about it, but I would retreat to the darkest spot in the corridor: there, pressing my forehead to the wall, I would swing my pigtails back and forth in time with the clock and trace the arabesques of the wall-hanging with my forefinger. "There you are, *Mädchen*, dreaming again," Richard would whisper as he approached me. He would lift me up in his arms, and I would stroke his bushy brow or his downy ear, I would smile in relief at his thick comforting mustache and his misty eyes behind their little round lenses. "I was in heaven, Grandfather," I'd softly tell him. "Next time, take me with you," he'd reply. Through the door of the drawing room came three chords on the piano and my grandmother's tart voice: "Richard, where in the world are you?" He would set me down on my feet, nod his head, and sigh, "Here we are back on earth."

One after the other, never together, we would return to the drawing room with downcast eyes, ready to face our pianist. She expected to be informed about the least thing happening in her house. Kindness and kissing had to take place in secret: she wouldn't have put up with such madness. I couldn't grasp why a man as strong as Richard would let himself be scolded or upset by Grandmother, or how she could get angry with such a gentle man. I wasn't aware that couples are often ill-matched, that one member can endure for an entire lifetime whatever the other inflicts on him, all because their paths had once happened to cross and because, later on, they let habit take them down a common road without ever suspecting that it might be the wrong one.

Grandmother was a formidable creature. Today I can laugh when I think of her terrible character and her noisy tantrums; at ten, I was very unhappy. I felt that I wasn't loved, that I was in fact victimized by this haughty, beautiful fury who'd never understood why her daughter had wanted a second child. One daughter was quite enough to worry about, and less of a problem when it came to arranging dowries and legacies. In short the second one—poor Alice—was a burden and was frequently told as much.

When she shook her pince-nez in her fine lace mitt as she railed against the maid or, perched on her chic high-button shoes and swinging her hips under her frilled satin skirts, passed by in a swirl of violet-scented air, I would be terrified and flatten myself against the nearest wall, praying she wouldn't notice my ink-mottled hands or the traces of jam at the corners of my mouth. Depending on the day, she might not notice me any more than the vase on the corner table; or she might stop short and subject me to a drill sergeant's inspection. I had a hard time hiding my anxiety, only glancing discreetly at the voluminous bosom heaving under its bangles. "Little slattern!" would fall from her pursed lips as she tapped my cheek with her lorgnette.

I was angry at Grandfather for never intervening on these occasions. He would look in dismay at his *Mädchen* from afar, with a discreet cough swivel the rocking chair toward the window, and disappear into his newspaper. Distractedly, Grandmother would turn right around in a rustle of silk, squeal, "Richard, shut up!" (he hadn't uttered a peep), and rush off elsewhere. By that time I would be in my mother's room upstairs, stifling my sobs in a velvet cushion.

The First World War has broken out. I'm ten years old. I don't really understand much. One day the Germans entered the town in their pointed helmets; they took prisoners. Since then, everyone's been talking about a catastrophe that will split Alsace in two. Such-and-such a girl's father disappears: he's gone to jail for being French; another friend's father, because he's Dutch. A third is shot as a spy, and I start crying—he was such a nice man! The inhabitants of Mulhouse have shut themselves indoors, afraid of neighbors that were so friendly the day before. You have to keep quiet, or at least not speak in French in the street anymore. That's what Grandfather says—sadly, since he's German. "*Auf Deutsch, Mädchen, nur auf Deutsch darfst du sprechen*": only German. No more "*Bonjour, Madame*," only "*Guten Tag, Gute Nacht*"; and how moody Grandfather has become! We speak Alsatian in order not to speak German. One day Grandmother made a serious mistake. Passing a lady in the street, she greets her with an all too resounding "*Bonjour, chère amie*"; they are both hauled off to the Hotel Central, converted into a prison for civilians, and there, in her finest visiting clothes—silk frock, fur stole, her very best hat with the ostrich feathers, and of course her gold pince-nez with the little chain behind her ear—pretty Mathilde has to spend an afternoon peeling potatoes under the mocking gaze of "that bunch of savages," as she later describes them. I can still see her coming home that evening, with her hat feathers ruffled and her pince-nez askew. We were left dumbfounded by the tale of her appalling day. She fell ill from the shame of it.

Later in the war. Ever since my father died, we've been living at North Station, where Grandfather is station superintendent (in German, *Obergüterversteher*). Mother isn't getting along with

Grandmother, who persecutes her. I don't understand why. I vividly remember that fateful lunch. Grandfather, red in the face, is mopping his brow with his napkin. The two women are arguing and yelling at each other across the table. My sister and I stare down at our plates. Suddenly my mother lets out a shriek and falls to the floor, a prey to violent shaking; while my grandmother, as she strides spluttering up and down, keeps repeating "It's play acting, nothing but play acting!"

Two days later, a mover's cart draws up in front of North Station. Mother has her furniture, packing cases, and piano loaded onto it, and the three of us go off on foot behind it. From behind the door come Grandmother's excessive sobs. On the sidewalk Grandfather stands in tears, waving his handkerchief.

Every Sunday morning he comes to see us at a run, kisses us, strokes our hair, slips a gold coin into Mother's pocket, gives us candy, and then leaves, with an eye on his watch: "Got to rush," he says, "she thinks I'm in church."

A pleasant memory: in our house on Rue de Nordfeld, on the floor above us, lived an extremely agreeable lady who seemed to me out of a fairy tale. She was Austrian, and she used to tell us scrumptious stories. There was also nothing she couldn't do with her hands. In two years' time she taught me the most complicated stitches in knitting and needlework—netting, tatting, macramé, lace. She had beautiful red hair and pink plump arms; she left behind her an aura of musk and pastry. In a cupboard hung with thick carved doors, she accumulated exotic preserves—green walnuts in syrup, stuffed prunes . . . In those days of war and famine, when one would see people falling down in the street from exhaustion, such wonders left us dizzy with pleasure. Where did she find these treasures? Later, Mother explained. It's true that on the stairs we often passed German officers and pretty ladies wearing a lot of makeup. It hardly matters. When our fairy godmother disappeared at the end of the war along with the Germans, I wept copious tears.

My mother's illness goes on for years. I have never seen her in good health, but always surmounting her pain to laugh and sing and make music with us. She dies at forty-four. It's impossible to describe my despair. My life has been a series of unacceptable deaths. Looking at her—so beautiful, so gentle—in her gown of black and white taffeta, smiling beneath her big feather hat, it's hard for me to believe that this young woman was my mother. I cradle her inside myself like my child.

I knew love once in my life, and it seared me to the bone. I did everything for this love, gauging the extent of my folly at every instant and with a precision not even the most perceptive among you could ever know. After forty years' existence (years filled with conflict), it is still intact. Look at me: I'm an old crippled lady and a widow, but I'm still the same love-stricken woman I was on the night of that dance, when it all started.

You understand: in 1920, in our provincial country towns, a girl of seventeen scarcely knew how babies are made. Thinking about it now, I wonder if a young man (even a chemist) knew much more about it. And it's exactly because of that that we conceived our son at our very first embrace.

But love, you say, love? We learned it together, and I promise you that our years of happiness would fill several chapters of a romantic novel. But then what, you ask, then what? Wait a moment, I have a headache. I have to stop and rest for a while . . .

(Afterward, I know, you'll refuse to remember: a first gap in your memory. Listen to me: you were a woman for whom motherhood was a consummation. With your ample, softly curved body, your broad, round hips and heavy breasts, you incarnated the happiness of fertility. You bore four children, you were a perfect mother, instinctive and animal, but you were also one of the innumerable women in whom the vocation of motherhood prevails over their intuitions as wives and lovers. All the same, there were no kinds of love that you couldn't have experienced and kept going simultaneously. But the one man in your life—the one who in the space of a single waltz won your heart and then, in the most conventional way imaginable, revealed your own body to you, teaching it caresses and love-making so as to make of you a docile, modest lover—never let you bloom with the impetuousness and violence that sets lovers free and would have enriched your tranquil tenderness with a little wildness. You became what he wanted: a domesticated woman, a submissive, model wife who could give free rein to her sensuality only in your relations with your children. You loved your offspring with true wildness—a good she-wolf, a jealous and voluptuous mother. Meanwhile, you relinquished to the male those powers you thought the male had been granted for all eternity. As wife, you were the traditional victim: you appeared when he wanted, you waited when you had to, you were satisfied when he so decreed.)

Think back to that night. Take a look at yourself—the immaculate wife, the adoring woman.

Rain is beating against the windowpanes. Alice has drawn the curtains so as not to feel the gaze of the wet, black night. Gusts of wind are sweeping leaves and twigs down the aisle of trees and against the door, where they will pile up in a spongy heap. She is sitting near the fireplace rereading *The Charterhouse of Parma*, her eyes all too often drifting from its pages to the hypnotic flames in the hearth. The children are asleep upstairs, quiet at last after a terrific pillow fight. A distant clatter of dishes reaches her from the kitchen. In a while the silent house will sink into the night.

She's waiting for him. This morning he said he was tired and wouldn't be home late. His research at the factory laboratory keeps him after hours later and later, more and more often. They don't go out anymore. They rarely entertain. She's bored. Her nights are long and dreary, punctuated with elaborate dreams. She is alone until the dawn that brings him home unheard, or else as a preoccupied man who in the middle of a sentence can disappear into deep, unmoving sleep.

She suddenly sees him in front of her. He is sitting on the sofa, leaning forward, his hands folded on his lap. He looks distraught. She must have dozed off.

"I've been speaking to you for five minutes now," he finally says. "The wind must have rocked you to sleep."

She straightens up and lights a cigarette. Her book slips from her knees.

"Talk to me, please. What's wrong?"

He seems at a loss. He starts to cry. She is so surprised at seeing tears streaming down his face, usually so proud and self-assured—these first tears running down his night-time, stubble-darkened face leave her so astounded that she is speechless, shifting her cigarette from one hand to the other before tossing it unsmoked into the fire. She hears him say, in clipped sentences:

"I'm thirty years old. I wanted to be a man. I thought I'd done what was right for that. I was wrong. I'm thirty. I haven't accomplished anything. I can't stand this well-planned life. I'm wasting my powers. This isn't what being a man means."

She doesn't reply. Given his state, he wouldn't hear her. She watches him get up, go to the sideboard, and take out the bottle of cognac. He's forgotten her and doesn't answer when she says, speaking less to him than to the night and to the barrier that separates them:

"I'm thirty years old. I've brought three children into your life. I wanted to be a woman who was your wife, and I thought I'd done what was right for that—devoting all my powers to planning a life that would be ours together. Isn't that being a woman and a wife?" The fire is dying gently. Rain still beats against the panes, but the wind has dropped. Once again she is alone in the room. Has she been dreaming? But the sideboard door hangs open, and a glass has marked the table with a damp ring. She stands up, closes the door, wipes off the brandy stain with her sleeve.

That night real loneliness begins for you. You are already resigning yourself to it.

How did you manage to adjust to this strange life of exclusion and ignorance that he forced on you?

. . . I don't know anymore. I see nights of waiting up, moves from one place to another, houses that are always comfortable, set in little parks on the outskirts of towns. There is no rebelliousness in me—perhaps it isn't the right moment, or it's my upbringing, I can't say. Three children . . . He goes away, and I wait for him, stubborn, stupid, in love. He's smart, too: he knows what I can stand better than I do, and he knows how to transform his returns into spontaneous celebrations in whirlwinds of talkative enthusiasm. I forgive him everything. He goes off again, sure of himself and of me. And it all starts over.

He was exasperated when I cried; so I learned to cry alone and to stop asking questions. I was one side of his life: a refuge, a reassuring image of family, a house where it was nice to stop over between battles. "The warrior's rest"—what a hateful expression! Well, I accepted it all.

His other side, with its outbursts and violence and excitement—his "man's life"—was utterly foreign to me, hidden by the darkness in which he wrapped it. Happy? No, resigned. In any case, ready to exercise all possible patience, to an insane degree: because there would always come a night, after I'd given him up, when he would radiantly emerge.

I lived a magnificent love story riddled with absences, never willing to acknowledge my disappointments. I've given up trying to understand. It's too long ago. Since then, the surf of war has rolled over us and left us differently wounded, differently stranded . . .

(Did you ever once break your silence and shout out loud? Did you ever ask yourself how those years could trample down your heart without having anything named or explained? There was the war, your second war. You accepted it as your personal destiny. You were utterly misled by it, you were the little Alsatian girl from the Great War, who didn't know where the frontier ran, whether on this side or that—it was like jumping from "rest" to "home" when you played hopscotch. Already as a child during those far-off gloomy years as an orphan in Mulhouse, you had built a rampart around you, with the world outside and your loneliness inside it. *Home!* In your little enclave you wanted tenderness to be your law; peace and love would rule there, and "Forget-me-not" would rhyme with "My love is in my arms." *Rest!* But into your forest of fir trees a man came looking for you. You thought you could enclose him within the circle you had drawn. *Home!* But the hunter had crossed woods and rivers, he spoke the language of love, then started speaking another one unknown to you. "*Bleib mit mir*" and "I love you" were no longer sung to the same patient tune. The hunter went out into the world. You stayed in your little enclosure. The world—its war and its violence—were not your concern. *Rest!* You hugged your little ones to you. You longed to shut their eyes on a perverted and shattered world and patiently teach them peace, love, and tenderness. You turned them into exiles from home and rest. Meanwhile, in the storm of events that you refused to understand, he was allying himself with the country of Grimm's fairy tales. Why should that have shocked you—you, the Alsatian, so familiar with the mingling of the two countries in their speech and their Christmastimes? The war disrupted all that. The vanquished hunter called to you for help; and from your forest haven you have leaped into chaos. You silently rescued him; but you never knew peace.)

When people spoke about the war, she would clench her teeth, shake her head, and stare out the window. She refused to collect memories of that dreadful time, as if the all-too-painful images of this particular past must be the first to fade from her invalid memory. So as not to answer questions, she would take refuge in her infirmity, whether deliberately or not: "Stop tormenting me, I don't know anymore, I have a headache." Or she would whisper, as if to herself, "You don't pass judgment on those you love. He paid for it. So did I."

It's inconceivable that she grasps so little, that the war passed over her head without her noticing anything, without realizing that the Germans were occupying France or that he—her hero—had picked the wrong side, the enemy side. "*Ach Gott, ich weiss*," I know that," she used to say impatiently, "but I'm a little bit German—and so are you." "But you were living in France, *carissima*, and your French husband was collaborating with Germans, in your own country." "My own country? I don't have a country. I'm Alsatian. In Alsace wars have always confused things, or shattered them. As in my own heart. *Verstehst du?* Can't you understand?"

I couldn't understand, but I watched her lean her head against the back of her chair and turn her moistened eyes toward the photographs over the piano; her bosom heaved, she stifled a sob, and a tear ran down her cheek, to be licked away with a flick of her tongue. As I kissed her, I asked her to forgive me for stirring up these memories, the "inexplicable" memories she wanted to forget. Taking my hand, careful not to mix up her words, she would murmur in a low voice, "*Hör zu, Mädchen*, listen, you were such a little girl. You don't even remember your eldest brother. He's another reason I can't talk any more about those awful years. Can you imagine my not resenting your father taking him off to Germany in '44 and letting him be killed in a bombing raid, and for nothing?" (she repeated more loudly, "for nothing"). "Don't you think he hated himself for it and ate his heart out over it, with all that time he had to think about it inside his prison walls? *Ach*, let it go, *lass das alles*. They're dead now, all of them." Her face resumed its sulky expression; she lowered her head. I knew she would say no more about the matter.

. . . My life is a worn-out fabric. In places it's threadbare, elsewhere it's unraveling. I try and sew it up again, patching holes, reknotting loose threads. Sometimes I re-embroider it, and then the colors get mixed up or overlap and make new patterns and shadows. What will you make of them? What will you learn about me? Often I myself don't know anymore, I shut my eyes, and it's all a jumble. I would have liked you to hold me close to your heart like a favorite book, we could have written the last chapter together, like the final movement of a symphony I would have had time to finish. But words escape me now and all too many pages will be left blank. The notes have flown off their staves and dance drunkenly inside my head.

I'm living out the end of a tale that I try to tell myself bits of every day. My memory is like my knitting, like the way I talk, full of holes, I keep trying to catch a dropped stitch or run after a word. I keep busy mingling what is past with what is passing, dressing the latter in the former's old clothes. I pass time by mending it. When I look at the lines in the wall, I know their every detail and blur by heart. I leaf through albums where each photograph is dated, where certain family scenes are even captioned. I advance, come back, jump ahead, dawdle, stop. I dream. I remember. I play back the images like ill-matched strips of a movie that I've never had time to edit . . .

The contours of the memories she had been gathering since earliest childhood gave birth to a kind of sentimental geography, with its plains and rivers, mountains and forests. As she traveled back through it, the images in which she recognized herself fused: she saw herself as the same person at ten, twenty, or thirty, or even later—someone forever preoccupied by this intimate geography and sacrificing everything to what in life was tender, emotional, or poignant.

Just as on a map of the world mountain ranges, seas, depressions, plains, and deserts are made legible by different hues, by the same token the zones of her life could have been distinguished by the colorings that time had bestowed on them. After a childhood essentially gray and a somewhat brighter, pink-fringed adolescence, her life as a woman, running along the shores of a dark green sea, passed through stages of pale blue, then red, and finally a violet that filled up the greater part of the map and extended its broad, uneven terrain toward the four points of the compass. The slender mauve strip of old age at last bordered the curlicues of a coast where no ship seemed ever likely to come ashore.

As she moved through the years, she took note of the colors of her travels, until the day came when she felt that her pace was slackening and that henceforth nothing in her imperceptible progress would be worth exhibiting in her museum. Then she locked its doors and settled down, keeping as her sole distraction the mute contemplation of her memories whose colors had faded and whose contours had grown vague, except for a very few: the livelier, sharper ones that were like oases in her desert and became the justification for daydreaming, for living under the spell of the past. Objects that had survived oblivion—snapshots, letters, curios, jewels, pieces of furniture—were her markers on a map whose outlines were more and more difficult for her to reconnoiter by heart. They filled up a storeroom of outdated props on which her memory could draw to illustrate the tales she kept indefatigably resuming.

So it goes with every solitary life as it decays, as it draws to its close. She knew as much. But her tenacity was stronger than her regret; and so she went her stumbling, hobbled way, afraid of only one thing worse—what she called soft-headedness.

"Better dead," she used to say. "Promise, promise . . ."

She would take my hand and squeeze it as her gaze went round the room. I would silently follow it as it explored her space, bearing witness to her lucidity and vouching for the reflections (sometimes deformed but enduring nevertheless) that her invalid's sense of reality retained for her.

She clung to her cloudy treasures. She was a sleepwalker frightened not so much of the night as of a twilight awakening in a shapeless world in which her fragmented memory would no longer find purchase or sanctuary.

Coma is the sleepwalker's final abode and refuge. Behind the shelter of her closed lids, she rambles. She is perhaps sailing upward among the branches of a blossoming tree on the swing her father let fly, laughing and tossing her head to shake loose the curls that have blown into her mouth. Or later, running in wide-cut slacks, she'll be leading her children down a mimosa-shaded path to a beach and its warm sand. An hour ago, perhaps, she saw the roadster pull up at the end of the drive, and saw the man get out and stride toward her to take her in his arms. Tomorrow, who knows, she may walk onto the stage of a gilded opera house and—"*Prendi: l'anel ti dono*"—sing Bellini's *Sonnambula*, gently falling asleep beneath her veils.

I go and see her every day. Three days already, and nothing has changed. Yesterday I saw the head doctor, a big bearded fellow, jovial and confident. With a handshake that almost floored me, he said before I could open my mouth,

"I think she's doing okay. I'm optimistic."

That was all I could find out. He was already charging into the next room. Anyway, in a hospital you never get to find out anything more. The nurse who was with him looked at me, disconsolately then almost angrily when I failed to register enthusiasm. I'd been spoken to—a rare privilege. What more did I want?

I have to take the elevator to get to her room. Dinner will soon be served. The corridors reek of institutional soup; its aroma cannot drown the bitter smell of disinfectant. As I let myself be carried upward in this wobbling crate (its dirty green paint flaking here and there), I hear the metallic tones of televised voices, amplified by the empty spaces through which they resound. On the fourth floor I have to cross a kind of lobby that narrows into a corridor. In the middle of this room a television set has been installed. In front of it, a number of pajama-clad convalescents, apparently neither seeing nor (especially) hearing them, are sullenly watching news reports blared forth from a world altogether remote from their own. Heads look round as I pass; a few nod sleepy hellos. They're starting to know me here.

In three days, three successive roommates have occupied the second bed in Room 7. All three smiled at me when I came in, responding to my hello, and their voices gave me a start. While I stood uneasily between the two beds, not daring to touch or kiss the sleeper in front of a stranger and unnerved by her noisy sleep (her raucous breathing was almost a snore), all three of them—happy at having a visitor and wanting to make the most of her—began talking to me since, after all, I couldn't talk to her. How old was the poor lady and what exactly had happened to her? Such a fresh complexion, such lovely skin, doesn't look sick at all! I obediently tell my story, grateful that one soul within these walls takes an interest in my case. All three also tried to cheer me up. The first has seen her eyelid move. The second, who in order to pass the time, she says, never stopped watching her, has caught her running her tongue over her dry lips. The third heard her groan while she was being washed—"A good sign, you know, it shows she can feel." On all three days I had left abruptly, no longer certain whom I'd come to see or on which table I was supposed to leave my flowers. Now I wonder what the fourth woman will be like today. It's evidently the custom here to vary the companions of adversity. Or is it because none of the three women could endure this proximity? I'll never know.

Just as I reach her room, a nurse comes rushing out, sees me, and orders: "Whatever you do, don't go in there!"

Through the open door I catch a glimpse of white smocks gathered around a bed in glaring light. Irritated, I follow instructions and lean against a wall, suddenly weak in the knees. The nurse comes running back, carrying some kind of appliance wrapped in a towel. I try to make her stop and talk to me but she won't hear of it: "Haven't got time, too much to do. They'll tell you when to go in." Night has fallen. Along the corridor, the windows overlooking the city are fitted with navy-blue squares streaked with small wavering lights. From behind the door I hear muffled voices and the clink of metallic objects set down on glass. Time passes. I walk over to a window and press my forehead against the cold pane. I'm going to follow headlights and count how many cars turn off at the intersection and how many drive straight through. A long line of yellow lights at one point comes to a halt. Why, it's a traffic jam. I'm in Paris—I'd forgotten. People are going home from work. They'll park their car, go upstairs, sit down in front of their television sets, and hear the same things I do—those voices at the end of the corridor, interspersed from time to time by more or less melodious snatches of music.

The shrill sound of a bell makes me jump. I turn around. A little red light is blinking above one of the doors. No other signs of life—except, over there, coming around the corner of the corridor, a skinny little boy who is hobbling toward me, his head swathed in bandages, his neck daubed with iodine. As he goes by, his two big eyes take me in indifferently, and he slowly makes his way toward the television set. It's time for the daily serial.

What if I left? No—they're coming out of the room. A racket of clattering glass and metal precedes them: still hurrying, the nurse is wheeling out a rolling table covered with bottles, receptacles, and bandages. There are three of them. I recognize the intern who received us, and the bearded man. They introduce me to the third, who wears glasses, is very mild mannered, and speaks with a strong

Central European accent. He's a surgeon. He does the talking, since he just has been practicing his craft.

"We had a little problem, but everything's fine. She was having trouble breathing. We performed a tracheotomy. You can go in."

Leaving me no time to stammer out two words, they turn on their heels and abandon me. For them the day is over—it's time to hop into their cars and go home if they're not to miss the eight o'clock news.

The little boy in the white turban goes by once again. The television set is silent. The long hospital night is beginning.

I can't just leave. She's waiting for me. I push the door open and glance at the second bed. It's empty. I'm alone with her; alone in the silence that is broken by the unusual hiss of breath that no longer follows its normal course. Her nostrils are pinched, her mouth half open; from the face whose eyes were already shut another trace of life is now gone. Breathing stops below the chin, at the place where they made their puncture, where I watch, as it rises and falls, trembling like a curtain in a breeze, a thin strip of gauze that conceals the artificial orifice with something like elegance.

To make her feel better, I tell her that I'll wrap lace round her bare shoulders and her mutilated neck. She isn't listening to me; she's deep into her night, lulled by the regular fluctuation of her breast under the sheet.

You aren't ugly yet. Your skin is soft, your hands are warm. Life is in you. Forget about the others. Let them practice their stupidities—they think they matter, but there's nothing they can do to you. Meet them with contempt. Annoy them, don't let yourself be woken up—they'd be all too happy. I'll come back tomorrow—I'll keep an eye on them. I'm not going to let them cut you up into little pieces. I won't mention what happened today, though. You weren't disfigured. The scalpel did its work discreetly, I can promise you that. The white veil wrapping the little incision is like a garland around your neck. Good night, my beauty. I'm going to steal away on tiptoe; steal away and dream about you.

Singing. No, you'll never sing again. Back there, that hadn't occurred to me.

I'd like to sleep, but I can't. I keep seeing you under the white light, with your throat slit. The trachea tricked. Where exactly are the vocal cords? Vocalizing: opera singer: diva: "*Casta Diva*" . . . In this night of mine, surrounded by a sleep that refuses to crawl into my seething brain, the voice of the *Diva divina soprana* takes shape and breadth, swells and dazzles. With a start I sit up and turn on the light, then feverishly grope my way: slippery record sleeves, liners, the record itself. Side 2. I've found it. I start it. *Norma*, and *la divina* Maria. Dusty. Take it easy, don't scratch the record, dammit. "*Casta diva . . .*"

Sitting on the floor, my head on my knees, hugging myself, a fetus suspended on cello strings, listening. The voice on the recording has to become one with the voice inside my brain, for the two of them to be at peace and transport me beyond the clouds to that vast house in which I imagine you. You sang this aria, long ago.

A night you'd spent waiting up—you had so many of those. Everyone else is asleep in the upstairs bedrooms. You come to wish me goodnight and tuck me in. The little ivory angel is swinging above my head, fastened to the stitched satin hood of the crib. I'm not hungry anymore. I'm snugly resting in my clean diapers and fresh sheets. You've left the nightlight on at the foot of the crib, the angel's shadow looms huge on the ceiling, my hands keep playing as they try to catch it. You kiss me—a butterfly wing—no, I'm not going to cry. You can go, floating on your velvet soles. The floor squeaks, you look back. I'm not crying. You leave the door open, and I listen to you going down the creaking stairs.

The living room is ablaze under all its ceiling lamps, which hold the darkness of the silent garden at bay. Night is tightening its grip around the walls of the house. Trees droop and fold their wings about your solitude. Branches brush like feathers against windowpanes, darkly outlining the world outside. Night is lying in wait for you: a fluid cavern in which you can feel at home, a familiar territory where you can at last find yourself.

He didn't come home tonight. He hasn't come home for months. He no longer tells you where or with whom he is, and you no longer bother to ask him. He has stopped leaving a number where you can call him in case of emergency—and what domestic emergency could match those urgent tasks he barely finds time to perform? You've trained yourself not to expect him any more, or at least you've deformed your expectation into believing that you no longer want him home. Those late-hour homecomings, his steps heavy on the gravel, a reek of drink and tobacco, eyes reddened, gestures slowed with fatigue, a muttered good morning. No: you don't want him here. Tonight you want to be alone, and sing.

You sit down at the piano. Your first notes flood the silence. Closing your eyes, you drift with them into dream. The living room becomes an opera stage, you move across it in magical unreality, through sleep's lacework screens, amid the gold and scarlet velvet of an Italian decor. You cleave the vibrant cello sky sustained by the unbroken silence of the huge theater, where a privileged audience sits breathless in an ambience of colors and silks.

You have risen to your feet. The few notes your fingers struck have let you soar in the midst of a muted orchestra, you can hear the chorus bearing you up as you begin your holy song, your arms outstretched like a sleepwalker stroking the waves, and your high voice scales the grief-stricken enchantments of "*Casta Diva*." If some interloper saw you now—draped in the folds of your satin robe, stepping blindly across the rug, priestess of an imaginary theater uttering a lament to the moon in a song that only you can know at this moment and whose music you alone hear—spying you, he would wonder, who is this woman? Is this a waking dream? Is she in pain? But you are alone and happy in your own self. Once again, coming back to earth, you sit down at the keyboard. You play the same aria through, and the piano now answers your voice and the orchestra that is fading away among the garden trees.

Did you ever sing Bellini? Did someone tell me about it or am I imagining things in my pursuit of you tonight, trying to give your voice back to you by making it sublime?

After those nights in my cradle when I listened to you, you gave up singing. Pianos still survived in your troubled life; but not singing—you didn't dare anymore. It would have demanded a buoyancy your body no longer felt. It would have overwhelmed you with too many regrets.

(On one occasion her dream almost did come true. It was shortly before the war. To keep her voice up, she was taking lessons in Lyon from an old spinster lady who introduced her to the great Panzéra. She performed Handel's "Largo" for him. He listened to her and said in all seriousness: “You should be a singer. Come to Paris. You can study with me, and later I’ll take you with me to America.” She thought she would faint for joy. Forgetting the world she lived in, where music’s role was a clandestine one, she said, “Of course I’ll come.” What an idea! By the time she’d reached home, she’d returned to her senses. How could she find the freedom to travel back and forth between Lyon and Paris, and then to America? And to become a *singer*? Her life had been established once and for all in a well-to-do house in the provinces, with her beloved children who couldn’t live without her and a man who would never tolerate her living without him—even if he was now no more than a shadow who arrived at daybreak and went to sleep beyond the reach of her warmth. The dream remained a dream. She didn’t become a singer; and afterward she only sang for herself, on those gypsy nights like the one on which I now imagine you; and I by now am asleep in my cradle, as innocent as Norma’s own children.

All at once you turn round and see him. He’s sitting in the leather armchair. Cigarette smoke is rising in a straight line from a motionless hand on the armrest. He is looking at you and smiling strangely. You begin feeling frantic. A cry of astonishment escapes you. How long has he been sitting there watching you? You hadn’t heard a thing: not the car, not the key in the lock. For a moment you wonder if he’s real; then he stretches out his hand. You go over to him and, with your hand in his, look at him gravely. There’s a gleam of curiosity in his eyes. He has just witnessed a performance that he hadn’t imagined. His wife not sleeping, not waiting up for him with her head bent over some saga or a piece of embroidery, a nocturnal woman moving in a space where there’s obviously no place for him. He suddenly finds that interesting. You feel like crying. You resent him for trampling on your dream, for coming in where he hasn’t been asked. As an onlooker he irritates you; and so when he asks you, "Sing some more for me," and squeezes your hand, the caress of his moist eyes exasperates you; but you give in. This man you love no longer sees you by day, he doesn't embrace you at night; but one evening he discovers another woman and wants to possess her. It's unfair. But you give in. You have no defenses—he's a man, you're a woman. You play your part and succumb.

You walk back to the piano like a robot. Your spine is stiff, your hands icy, your voice trembles. "No," he says dully, "the aria you were singing." You obey; and while you strain to unravel the broken arabesques of the great lunar song of Norma the priestess, you endure the pain of nakedness, more naked than ever before, unbearably so, under the beam of a desire that you have not sought. Tonight you won't sleep alone. You will find no pleasure in that. He'll never know. He's not one to be woken up by a stifled sob. His sleep is always deep and refreshing. It's the secret of his health.

La Callas has now fallen silent. Norma has mounted the pyre, drawing Pollione, her lover and the father of her children, into the purification of death. The red curtain falls on my dream; and on yours. I never knew you as the brown-haired young woman with the graceful walk; the nostalgic singer of sleepless nights in the long-forgotten houses of childhood; the young woman all satin and velvet, in love with another life and with a man she couldn't hold within her fragrant dwelling; the young, exquisite, pure-voiced woman whose griefs were secret.

How I would have loved you then! How I would have done everything to keep the luminous power in your eyes from dissolving in miserable floods of tears! But I came too late. Trouble was there already, running stealthily and deep beneath your sunny spaces. You hair had started turning white; you no longer sang. As far back as I can relive my memories of you, I see you as weariness incarnate: mother, wife, and woman. In the silence of this night broken only by the wheezing underneath your gauze choker, I keep telling myself—biting my lips so as not to cry it out—I tell myself it's a good thing you're asleep at last and no longer realize how near your life was to its end.

But then why, why do people always say this about the dead? Why does everyone look for reassurance in this final silence, this final collapse, telling themselves over and over that the dead will be at peace, that their underground sleep is an eternal rest? What if it isn't?

Here I am, rocking helplessly back and forth on my bedroom carpet with my head against my knees. I've abandoned you as you slide into the mists. You aren't struggling any longer, you couldn't care less about your body—you don't live there anymore, they can do what they want with it. And I'm letting them. I'm hanging on your breath, waiting for it to fail, praying whomever or whatever or nobody at all but praying all the same that it too will leave this body of yours that has become the cumbersome relic of one life, of one more life.

I know nothing of childhood sorrows—those fugitive events that we later decide to call traumas when we try to define the emotions that assail us, those little things that turn us into helpless big babies, those trivial dramas whose importance is so vital that later on we collect them to try and explain the grown-ups we think we have become.

Those sorrows passed me by. I know I must have cried, but the tears left no aftertaste. Like the drawings, paintings, and festoons that illumine our early years and for which we so quickly lose the gift, like the fairytale characters that we invent to keep the prosaic adult world at a distance and who disappear when we start playing at growing up, the secret of those tears lies buried somewhere in the museum of childhood.

Any number of events that punctuated my early years might have torn their fragile sails. But I was lucky: the crises took place behind closed doors, in rooms where grown-ups met at night and spoke in hushed voices. I never went to sleep without a song, without a smile. And I was spared that multitude of petty accidents—the little miseries that leave such big scars, the shocks that so sadden the heart.

Whatever sorrows there may have been are now forgotten; or perhaps I let them sink and disappear forever in the liquid depths of her eyes.

The truth is, I lived with a woman, with a mother, who chose to take every sorrow on herself. She walked slower so that we could run faster; she stifled her own tears so we wouldn't forget how to laugh.

When I was a child, she was still young. To me she looked beautiful; and she was. Beautiful and sad. Living her sorrow like a vocation. From time immemorial. Having held onto something and lost it; having loved only to suffer. But I didn't know that, not then or for a long time after. One talks about people's fate only after they die; or, if they're alive, only if they've collapsed under too great a weight of accident and grief. She hadn't collapsed: she was simply bowed down by weariness—a weariness that I tried to dispel by making her laugh and by acting silly (no doubt irritating her often enough). A weariness whose origin I didn't understand. A few silver hairs showed in the brown around her forehead; her smile sometimes seemed strained; when she spoke with others, I used to count the sighs that slipped out between sentences.

I loved her passionately. She was my whole life. And since love is selfish, I was unaware of everything outside the two of us; I was incapable of imagining that she might need anyone besides me.

There was no man around the house. I'd always seen her alone: how could I suspect the obvious truth that a woman may need a man in her life? Wrapped in this solitude, to me she was perfection. How could I guess that the man we visited once a week (he's your father, you must love him, and I certainly did love him but I didn't miss him: he'd never been around), how could I guess that this man had a place in her heart, that from the beginning his absence had secretly haunted her nights, that her latent sorrow, her sighs, and the traces of tears each morning were due to him?

He was the one she had loved since that very distant time when I didn't know her, that realm of unreality where she had led her life without me: her past. It had the pastel color of the dresses she had never thrown out, crêpe de chine and flowery silk, kept now in cardboard boxes as relics of another life. Would she ever wear them again? "I don't know," she used to say, "probably not—they'd be out of fashion, and much too pale." At the time, she dressed in dark colors—a worn purple dress, or a black suit that she used to rough up with a wet brush to revive its nap. I would have liked her to be more sinuous, fluttering in muslin, more made-up, laughing behind a frothy veil. That was how she appeared in certain snapshots from "before," where she seemed to me as beautiful as Garbo. "But I can't," she'd say to me. "Later, maybe, when life is different . . ."

Later meant: when he comes back. For his return, other clothes as well had been stored in mothballs: sumptuous nightgowns and negligees he had given her during the first years of their marriage. No one else would ever see her attired in pure silk and beaded satin.

Meanwhile, while she waited for him, she slept alone, in a bed next to mine. If I was harassed by a nightmare, it was a woman's voice—her own—that reassured me. The only warmth I knew was hers; I didn't realize that a man, too, might have arms in which to enfold me. I didn't need him. I wasn't all that jealous, but I think I would have preferred him not to come back.

When I was a little older, I understood (at least I think I did) that to love someone involves more than just getting—you have to make some sacrifices, too. So I began wishing that she could have her man back, since she seemed to want it so much. We waited for him together. She talked about his travels, his ill-fated adventures, his love for her. I imagined him as a valiant warrior issuing triumphant from all his battles. For me, a man was exactly that, a magnificent adventurer, and it was all the more wonderful to live at a distance from him the longer he stayed away. However, one day his homecoming was announced.

The theatrical setting in which I had thus far moved with all the lightness of an insect flitting in the sun soon lost its dreamlike air: it acquired a denser, papier-mâché consistency, and less sparkling colors. The walls were closing in. He would soon be here. She waited for him with such anxiety that I thought, he's the Messiah, he's bound to perform a miracle when he arrives. He'll give her back her youth, her buoyant shoulders, he'll erase the weariness around her eyes, she'll never be afraid again, and she'll be able to buy new clothes.

She had the patience of a sea captain's wife. The years had gone by like so many bitter waves, bearing gleams of hope, disappointments, swirls of fruitless endeavors, carrying away expectations and regrets for a few more wasted seasons, in a slow ebb of passing days that leave nothing behind them but greater loneliness.

Her man wasn't at sea, struggling against the unbridled elements. Other dreams and a very different sort of venture had left him behind bars where he was serving, as they say, his sentence. An amnesty would transform his life term into a ten-year exile between four walls.

Today, however, I'm looking at her. As I scrutinize this face that, as it sets, is molding the definitive features of its own mask, I know one thing: what I want to see in it is not events themselves but the wounds they've etched. What I can discern in this face is a reflection of ten years of waiting and the shock of a homecoming that, although heralded so often, no longer seemed part of conceivable reality.

One day at the beginning of spring, nonetheless, we heard a resounding "He's free!"—a ringing, happy signal that echoed through the burgeoning branches. When an old, old dream becomes brutally real, it's hard to find a place for it in our daily lives. We think we are living in an anguish of waiting: later, we realize that it was the waiting that nourished our lives. In just such a way darkness envelops and soothes the prisoner—send him out into the daylight and he'll fall down blinded.

She had lived through ten years of painful separation sheathed in her prickly fidelity. How will she sustain the shock of reunion, when the door opens onto blinding daylight? Whom will she see in front of her? When, after ten years, two solitudes meet, what can they say to one another?

You have to see her that morning, a dry morning in Lorraine, pale and stiff in her black coat as she confronts the eastern spring, which is sharp enough to still feel like winter. Look at her, erect, sure of herself, scarcely shivering as she approaches the barbed wire of the sprawling prison camp where he has spent his last two years of detention. She is about to act out her lovers' rendezvous. Her captive is being restored to her. Is my hair in place? she wonders. Am I still beautiful? Will he find me attractive tonight? Look at her in the pale April sunlight, standing immobile in front of the huge gateway, her gaze hard, indifferent to the two guards who are watching her. Look at her imperiously knotting her scarf, taking her compact out of her handbag, clicking it open, considering herself impartially, then powdering her nose, reddened by the wind. She thinks: I was forty. I was wife and mother, my body was soft and strong, and at the end of your crusades you enjoyed coming back to me and my unalterable love. Now I have to disguise my gray hairs and the circles under my eyes. Will you recognize my body, or even the way I look at you? Won't we frighten each other—it's been so long since we moved and thrilled and slept together? Which of us can consider the other without trembling, without swallowing his tears, without crying his distress in the depths of his soul? Which of us will be the first to break down?

The gate opens. She sees him in the distance, in his tightfitting old brown leather windbreaker. A small canvas bag swings from one arm; in the other he carries his white hat. He walks slowly and jerkily, counting the yards that separate him from a newfound world of other people. He weaves across the barren ground as if testing his legs, like a sailor ashore after a long crossing. The cigarette to one side of his smiling mouth trembles a little. He's getting nearer. She thinks: it's his way of walking—he hasn't changed, her lips are frozen in a vague smile she cannot control, her hands are clenched inside pockets too small for them. Today's the day he's coming back into my life, erect, proud, almost serene, as if he'd never had a worry. And now a woman who is me is about to fling herself into the arms of a man who is you, and for so long there's been nothing, no warmth, no touching or lovemaking, for so long, my love, nothing but emptiness.

We shall never know, as from a yard away she beheld the man's face wavering through her tears, whether what she thought was "At last!" or "It's all over."

A man had come back home. Someone kept whispering in my ear that the drama was ending, that we should start singing; but I had lost my voice, and my least movement bumped me against a blank wall. Childhood was over. I suffered my first heartache.

Only words, you say? Then listen to what happened next. In my day (I don't mean to sound old) children were generally kept uninformed about adult behavior. I had no idea, for example, that a man and a woman embraced when they made love. I knew of course that I had emerged from my mother's belly, but I never thought of asking how I'd gotten inside it. So when this man had no sooner had a foot inside the door than he moved into my room and, what's more, into the bed of the woman I loved, and when this sighing, perfumed woman began coming to wish me a hurried goodnight on the dining room sofa, I did not applaud.

Heartache took hold of me and would not let me go. It was a bitter cloud of something like the hissing smoke chemists induce when they let a drop of acid fall onto certain compounds. The cloud took shape surreptitiously in a part of my body that was hard to localize but felt like the bottom of a well. It proliferated with the speed of a poisonous mushroom, sending up shoots from the solar plexus into my nostrils, stopping for variable intervals in my throat, where it thickened into cottonlike consistency. It took me a long time to recognize it as heartache. When something nameless suddenly grips you, before trying to identify it you wonder how to chew or spit out or vomit up the thing that's choking you. It can leave you nauseated for weeks on end. That's what happened to me.

I tried mollifying it, I tried watering it with my tears so that it would drain away more easily. But it persisted, especially at night, at the moment when my mother was leaning over me. Because she looked sadder and sadder. Something's wrong, I thought, something's definitely wrong. But what more can she want? I didn't dare ask her, afraid she'd start breaking down and make my heartache even stickier. I contented myself with breathing in her smell and stroking her shoulders and hair. I had not been properly informed. I had not been told that between men and women things can, sometimes, go wrong.

He'd come back; he'd performed no miracle. A sense of injustice overcame me. Little by little my sorrow changed to bitterness, as I watched a melancholy appear in her countenance, a distress in her eyes, that should never have been there—not after the hero was home. She'd promised as much.

I couldn't stand it any longer. One fond night—we were alone, on the brink of sleep, stroking one another's hands, trying without admitting it to recover a lost complicity—one night of fumbling tenderness, I asked her to smooth away the two little wrinkles on her forehead and explain what was causing them.

"So you noticed!" she said to me. "I know I *ought* to be happy. It's nothing, it won't last. Just a little leftover heartache I've hung onto, it's still resisting our bodies' warmth. It's difficult, you know. It takes time."

("Heartache"—you, too? It can't be so. It can't be the same thing. And when you speak of time, your eyes tell me that time is what you no longer have.)

"It's late," she said with a sigh, "you've got to sleep. You'll see: later . . ." Her gaze floated away. I don't like it when she looks into the future. I don't want her to leave me for the shores of old age, where people land laden with knowledge and experience, so they think, but most of all with regrets. "You'll see," she went on. "Things are never the way you'd imagined them. Sometimes waiting for an event is so overwhelming that when it happens you have no strength left for it."

Perhaps I would see, later. I didn't much care. What I saw then and there was a woman exhausted of her substance, almost invisible, adrift amid sorrows that were draining the color from her cheeks.

I would have liked to restrain her, but she had already gone too far, and I hadn't yet strength enough. Between us stretched the expanse of years, that incessant, unswerving stream that no bridge—not even the greatest love—can span.

What I would see later is something you never dared teach me, because life means we each are left to our own fate: that heartaches are solitary and, like us, live out their lives to the end.

I count the days. They follow each other, identical autumn days, differing only by a few minutes' more grayness in the morning and darkness at night. Winter is approaching. Season is following season; we keep on; nothing stops. Snow will soon extend the horizon, already soft and white, toward which we make our way together, you as sleep's passenger, I as your discreet traveling companion.

I get up in the morning to wait for night. I go up and down stairs; I walk along corridors; I notice passing faces and exchange a word or two; I walk in streets, I cross intersections, I look at my watch and the sky and the passersby going their way, and I live only for the moment at nightfall when I can board your ghostly train.

Beyond the windows of our strange railroad car, distant sounds emerge and lights blink in a city we never stop crossing. It doesn't matter where you're taking me: I'll always be in attendance. I hold your hand in mine and close my eyes. Your cruising speed never varies; your itinerary has apparently been settled. Season will be linked to other seasons, and you will still be there, unchanged, lying beneath the folds of your sheet like an embalmed saint in a glass shrine.

From time to time the door opens, and a white shape approaches. A face smiles at me, a voice speaks from afar and fails to reach me. I answer aimlessly. The person bends over you, prods you, tests you, checks the workings of the ever more numerous instruments connected to your body. If they lift up the sheet, I look away. Finally they write something down at the foot of the bed and go out. The two of us are once again alone in our silent compartment, and our journey resumes.

A bell is ringing. There are voices in the corridor. At the far end of the floor the television has been turned on. And here I am, standing at the foot of a hospital bed, aware of the cold metal bar against my palms. Discouraged. I too have been getting literary and let myself be carried away by images of travel. Euphemisms, clichés. When all one has to do is open one's eyes.

In a hospital bed, a woman is dying. Her heart—her undiminished heart, that excellent machine—is holding out and keeps beating, beating. But all the rest, her whole body, is gently letting go, unalarmed, in time with her breathing, sometimes hoarse, sometimes wheezing, sometimes stopping for one, two, three seconds, and I jump up and lean over her; then it starts up again—rattling and unsteady perhaps, but functioning. In other rooms other women are dying. It does not matter who they were or what their lives were like. Together they are withdrawing from them. We who are alive watch them leave; and our efforts will not save them from oblivion.

It must be late. I can't stand these walls any longer. I grab my coat and head for the door.

From behind closed eyes she calls me. I'm laughing as I turn around and hold out my hand, and then we're running together down a station platform under a sunlit high glass roof.

I'd taken my time when I left the lycée, thinking I'd wander down to the Jardin des Poètes, kicking my way slowly through the brown and yellow horse-chestnut leaves, some damp and soft, others brittle. I didn't feel like going home; I knew she wouldn't be there. The silent piano would be shut, haughtily withdrawn into its corner, proud that no one could stroke it but her. Awaiting her return, it would become silvered with dust. No one would disrupt the orderly disposal of scores lying neatly piled on its gleaming animal's back. The thick bunch of short-stemmed tea roses that she had placed on the black surface would listlessly let fall its petals, and nobody would clear them away.

I had set my books on the ground. Sitting on a step outside the high bay windows of Lycée La Fontaine, I was pulling up my bobby socks, which kept disappearing into my moccasins and wadding themselves disagreeably under my heels.

A taxi has pulled up to the curb. Its door opens and a long leg emerges, my gaze starts at the point of a pump, moves up to a black glove and a flannel suit that I've seen before, and then, in the sunlight trickling through the last leaves of the horse chestnuts, her silver locks and red lips. She smiles and gaily calls my name. I rush toward her. She's holding her dark-red felt hat in one hand. She kisses me. She smells good.

"Hop in. You're taking me to the station. I'm catching the Mistral—the concert in Aix is tonight. It's a private affair, evening dress, very chic."

You'll play them Liszt and Chopin, languidly, sheathed in black-onyx bugle beads. You'll try to ignore the hothouse plants they've dutifully placed around the piano and the imperceptible smell of sandwiches that reaches you from the sideboard, floating above the dinner jackets and the décolletéd backs and mingling incongruously with the slightly too heady perfumes of these ladies.

My fashion forecast makes her laugh.

"Anyway, I'll be thinking of you," she tells me. "I'll close my eyes . . . When my fingers start running over the keys, you know I'm in heaven."

"Take me with you!"

"Don't be silly," her voice sings to me. The amethyst that has swiveled around her finger scratches my cheek as she strokes it. The taxi drops us at Gare de Lyon outside the departure entrance. We barely make it to her train.

Tossing me her muslin scarf, she nimbly eludes me. It smells of Cinq de Molyneux. I don't like seeing her leave—I'm never sure she'll come back. She knows; and so we've our game, this ritual of an object proffered to me at the last minute. She never refers to it ahead of time, but in the instant of farewell, at the last possible moment (as to avoid displays that would devastate us), she spins round, laughter spills out of her, and I receive as keepsake some tiny thing—a handkerchief, a trinket, a tube of lipstick. One day when she was leaving on a long trip, she threw her amethyst ring out the car window. By the time I'd retrieved it, she was gone; in the distance I could see her bare hand waving from the window.

The train starts up. I press the scarf to my lips. My eyes bid good-bye to the mischievous, tender smile behind the window.

A nurse comes into the room. She is astonished to find me still there, with my coat over my shoulders.

"No change," she remarks, just to say something. "But you see how clear her skin is."

I smile my thanks and cast a last look at the hands lying limp on the sheet. The edema is worse. Her fingers are swollen. On her left third finger, the wedding band and the engagement ring studded with a little diamond have sunk into the flesh.

She never went to Aix. I dreamed that. I dreamed the dark-red hat, the Liszt and Chopin, and the smile behind the train window.

It was a rainy autumn day. Sticky with mud, the horse-chestnut leaves lay sodden on the sidewalk, or piled up on the circular gratings at the foot of trees, or swam down gutters swept along by the street cleaner's broom. The taxi's windshield wipers squeaked, its tires hissed their way through puddles. I held her weary hand and twisted the ring around her finger.

"Why are you going—you're so tired? You hardly knew this woman. They can bury her without you."

"Hush. I won't enjoy it, but it's a token politeness. He asked me to. An old friend has been widowed, and he wants to show his loyalty."

"Why can't he be polite on his own, without making you take a trip to another cemetery? Don't go."

Her soothing smile and drooping eyelids tell me: "You're right, I'm worn out, but I'm going all the same." I resent her weakness, her submissiveness. Why does she always yield, obey, and keep silent?

Her legs look beautiful in their black stockings. She shivers and tightens the high collar of her Persian-lamb jacket. She's wearing a little too much make-up. The silky pink of her cheeks heightens the pallor of her forehead.

The taxi leaves us at Gare de Lyon outside the departure entrance. It doesn't matter where the train is taking her. It will be somewhere in the country, under fine October rain.

As I watched her face gliding behind the rain-lashed window-pane, I knew she was in danger. I didn't want her to leave. I called out to her, but the train was under way. I never again saw the woman from whom I parted that day on a station platform.

It happened without warning. On the night of that damned funeral I was supposed to meet her at the station; but in mid-afternoon the telephone rang. I listened impassively as a voice declared that childhood was swiftly deserting me, that my adolescence was entering a tunnel, that never again would I believe in God or anything else, that henceforth I would be alone—alone in the morning, alone at night, alone with others or without them. But you have to show pluck. That's the way life is, the voice continues . . . The voice went on wobbling and crackling as it told its story, with gaps of silence—"Can you hear me? Hello? Can you hear me?"—but with no awareness that sorrow, the vast sorrow that pummels, levels, and devours, thick and searing as lava, was in deafening spasms seeping through my ear and swiftly filling my mind before inundating me entirely, from the depths of my heart to my fingertips.

She had collapsed while drinking coffee. "How? Why? Could you repeat that? Could you start from the beginning?" "Of course," the voice said patiently. "She was feeling tired, no more than that. She said she would go back to Paris as soon as possible. She wouldn't lie down. 'At least have lunch with us'—so she joined us, and everything was fine. We went into the living room for coffee. I hand her a cup. She sets it on the armrest of her chair, opens her bag, takes out her cigarette holder, and I light her Chesterfield for her. We're talking and, all of a sudden, halfway through a sentence, she sits up and stares at me. She grabs her chair and the coffee falls to the floor. She yells, 'No, no, not that!' and sinks back unconscious."

I hang up. I know what happens next.

They called a doctor, the doctor called an ambulance, the ambulance took her to a hospital. A hospital like any other: white smocks, white rooms, ether, formalin, cafeterias, rolling tables going down white corridors, coma.

What a disaster, felled by a stroke, when she was barely getting old! Doctor, at her age, can she recover?—Hard to say, hard to say. And if she does, you know, she'll be damaged goods. All right, it's simple. Imagine a torrential cloudburst. Rivers are flooded, fields under water, trees carried away. Sooner or later the river returns to its bed, and the muddy earth sops up the water. But that takes time, and there's been considerable damage. The flooded field was her brain. Something gave way, behind one eye. A dike broke. It may not kill her, but it may turn half her body to wood. It's called hemiplegia—a Greek word meaning "half stricken." The way nature works is that one day it strikes without warning and takes away half your body. You have to manage with what's left.

For many long days she knew nothing. Thick fog engulfed her entire being. We took turns at her bedside, waiting for a sign, a word, a look. I was very young then and interested in explanations. I kept repeating to myself: they've wrecked the woman I loved. Things would never be the same again. In my sky there was a stain that nothing could remove.

I was at her bedside, her lifeless hand nestled in my hands. A finger suddenly stirred, as if knocking at my door. An eyelid slid upward, as if a window were being opened, I heard her voice: "I'm on the way." I believed her, and she kept her word. Day after day, she made her way back to us.

. . . I remember, she said, I went on a long journey. I wasn't in pain. I was floating among voices inside a glass cage. The voices, velvety as feathers, beat softly against my walls. I recognized that you were calling me. But I felt like taking my time and not complying too quickly. I wasn't frightened. More than once I felt tempted to leave you. I was being called from the other side, too, where vast domains of iridescent light stretched away into infinity and the air was filled with beautiful clear carols and soothing requiems. Whenever I started thinking, my thoughts were liquid and warm, like milk flowing comfortingly through my veins. Slipping over to that far side seemed so easy. But again I heard your voices, and I made my choice.

People are known to speak of someone being "far gone"—it's true. I was very far from you. I saw them all once again. They used gentleness and charm to draw me toward them, circling around me like great birds. I held out. It wasn't yet time to follow them.

I relived the earlier moments when I'd almost left, when I most wanted to leave. I saw my mother at my bedside in Mulhouse, during the war. There was no milk to be had anywhere, and the only thing that could save me was fresh milk. All day long she scoured the countryside, to return at nightfall with a little jug hidden under her cloak. I recognized the limp feeling when all the pain drains out of you, the longing to topple over into a nothingness soft as feathers and slide dizzyingly down toward infinite ease: like that night when I'd waited and lain awake long enough, when I almost took off, just wanting to sleep and sleep. But the horse's hooves, the carriage wheels on the cobblestones outside the front door, and a snowy chill woke me; and your voices. The carriage went off without me. Not yet.

I made my way back—a long pilgrimage. Once again, after the war, I took the train at Strasbourg with my grandfather to visit the country of his childhood. Once again I saw the Germany of my dreams, the big garden, the enchanted grounds, the ivy-mantled house, blond children running in the meadow, and me, all shyness in my black stockings and starched skirts. For a long time I kept hovering over Germany, that ill-fated land, I saw Berlin, its blood-colored flags snapping in the wind, and Ulm under the bombs. I walked through the great green-and-white graveyard and almost lay down among all the unknown dead, they spoke to me and begged me to stay. But I went away. I myself might have fallen down the Stairs of Death, the *Todesstiege* at Mauthausen, and been drowned with them in the blind pond below the cliff, with their screams in my ears. Why did I take so long to see all that? Germany, ill-fated Germany that runs in my veins.

The dead are tremendous: their voices are beguiling, and their loneliness is vast. If a living being passes near them and wonders which path to take, they mislead him. They reveal the light of their day and hide the boredom of their darkness. They do not show him the subterranean mud into which they sink, or speak of frozen earth and roots tangling with their bones. I remembered my body, and I came back . . .

And yet her body . . . She had gone anywhere she wanted, tireless and proud; she would now be a woman in a chair. But what a woman! There was a great store of youthfulness in her, and it gave her strength to meet this challenge: as soon as she had emerged from her mists, she took stock of herself. She had nothing but contempt for the lapsed cells in her brain, and she treated with scorn the part of her that she now dragged around like a millstone. "I still have my good side," she would say gleefully, "the side my heart is on." Her heart brought her to an unhoped-for semi-recovery, like a near-dead tree that puts forth one crazy branch, struggling skyward to make it look like a tree again. Of course, it's no longer the same tree, but it's alive. She was no longer the same woman. She was fifty years old.

. . . You'll never know (she said) my shame at growing old—growing old badly, all askew, split down the middle. What a trap I set myself! At first I didn't understand. Coming back was wonderful—opening up little by little, seeing the sky and trees, hearing voices again. I loved catching the look on the doctors' faces, astonished when I made unexpected progress. I was, as they say, getting back on my feet. I didn't take many steps.

One day I found myself at a crossroads, out of breath, and I knew that that was as far as I'd go. An old woman was waiting for me there, jeering and wobbly, and I knew she wouldn't let me out of her sight. Ever since, she's been pursing me with her cane, taunting me whenever I glimpse her in a mirror. I hate her when I hear her dragging her wooden leg down the corridor, when she deserts me with a snigger in mid-sentence, when she keeps me from following the story you're telling, when she knocks over the glass on the tablecloth with a helpless, clumsy gesture, or when she loses interest and leaves me in front of my bowl of soup with the corner of my mouth soiled with food I can't feel. She makes me weep with rage by refusing to tie my shoelaces or by dropping my stitches or muddling the lines on the page so I can't even write my own name.

Don't you think I notice you smiling at her? Or using all your patience when she's sulky or unable to understand what you're saying? You don't get irritated, you repeat your sentence most politely, and she assents, the hypocrite, nodding the disheveled head I'd so carefully combed that morning, but the poor crazy woman doesn't understand a thing. You don't hear me then, screaming and trying to burst through her shell. I sometimes feel like killing her, but she's stubborn, she won't let me. She's the stronger of us two, and she hangs on, smiling oh so sweetly at you, picking up her cane, simpering while she takes you to the door.

You'll never know how I suffer from her hold on me. I can't speak to you anymore—she's even stolen my voice. I keep struggling hopelessly and watch her keep gaining ground, settling into my furniture, my clothes, even my head. She's taken over the little life I had left. My memories are all hers now. I've had to give up. I've had to make peace with her old bones.

We're nothing more than "a waiting" now. One and the same old age in which she's disguised me in spite of myself, and soon one death toward which she's leading me step by step. Meanwhile, to pass the hours, we knit, we rewind the balls of wool spilling out of the workbasket next to our chair, we regild old images and string them into necklaces.

At nightfall, the old woman finally forgets me for a while. I fall asleep, alone with my dreams. I shut my eyes, and there is the woman that deserted me on that autumn day when I collapsed. I walk, I run, I never get sick, I'm never hobbled with crutches. I speak flawlessly, I sing—above all, I sing and feel the notes rippling under the fingers of my unknotted hands. Can you understand why I want to sleep forever and never wake up, never have to see her again, sitting on the edge of my bed in the morning, showing me my face in the mirror she's holding up to me, telling me, "All right, it's a new day, follow me!"? . . .

. . . Everything was diminishing, she said. I was less and less in my body. Everything was receding. When you came to see me, you thought you were talking to me, but your voice couldn't carry as far as my glass cage. You thought you were holding my hand; you didn't feel the ice seeping into it. Everything was slipping away. I was barely present; but I saw everything. You can't imagine what it cost me to answer you, to move from armchair to table, from table to door, to hint at the gesture that would allow you to think that I was still there, unchanged; to repeat one day what I'd managed not to forget from the day before; to continue tomorrow what I had miraculously succeeded in starting today. Before that—at a time now dreadfully distant—each day coming in its turn was a victory over my numbed body and kept it going in spite of itself, like a pendulum. But before long the revolving hours turned into a chain of burdens, leading nowhere. My impetus had broken down; my desires had gone. The old woman in charge of me got as tired as I was. She stopped speaking. She was content simply to wag her head or suddenly brandish her cane at the wall. Then she would sink back into her torpor, resting her head on the antimacassar. She was waiting for me. I knew she wouldn't wait much longer. I had nothing left, except a longing to fall asleep at night and not worry about anything. I wish I could have disappeared without a sound, without frightening you . . .

The hardest thing is to keep going—without reason or purpose. I keep going like a smoldering fire, like stagnant water, like an incurable disease. I keep going for nothing. You can't imagine my sadness as I hear life leaving me, like a great heart no longer beating for me; seeing you fade away. Without even the courage to stretch out my arms to you, or call you, or say "I'm going, hold on to me!" You will never know my terror . . .

Autumn has been lovely this year. Along the avenues, pale sunlight flickers through the last shriveled leaves that cling tenaciously to the branches of the horse chestnut and plane trees. Paris loafs, gilding its dustiness in a dawdling, late October mildness. The dry-backed streets have apparently forgotten that vast rainy winds can suddenly darken the sky and sweep them roughly with their sodden wings. Chrysanthemums bloom on sidewalks, condemned through the ages to bow their disheveled heads over tombstones. Tomorrow comes November, initiating mourning.

On the first of November, people think of their dead and deck them with fresh flowers—a custom that sets graveyards ablaze. Later, wreaths and bouquets droop, thick-leaved plants scatter themselves mournfully over the stones, drying up in wind, rotting in rain. The great parks, animated once a year, soon fade and bog down and, when frost at last congeals them, look like vacant lots, or like soiled tablecloths after a wedding breakfast. The dead have had their party. What have they got to complain about? They don't complain; and stones reclaim their bareness amid the slow decomposition of plants.

City people have too little time now to think of their dead. Once their feast day is over—a handful of flowers on a stone slab—they shut themselves warmly indoors and forget them until the next autumn and the next chrysanthemums. Why go wandering around those vast suburban fields, hardly—between having to park the car and a bleak skyline of dormitory cities—conducive to meditation? Those who remember once a year and only walk through these tree-lined ways under November skies will never know the melancholy of all those wilted graves, where here and there plastic flowers emerge, garishly inappropriate, earth-splotched by rain but still obstinately dotting the ground with their artificial hues. They will never know the solitude of these little mounds of flowers, tributes of the day to the latest newcomer laid here to rest. On him funeral bouquets and wreaths have been heaped under gold-lettered purple bands, with nothing to spare for his neighbor, all alone and bare next to this pile of greenery, which will itself start rotting soon enough.

I often go for walks in graveyards. I sit down on a marble ledge and read names and dates, or I muse over faded medallions of a young soldier slain on the field of battle, of the lovely Adèle who died in childbirth, of a baby wrapped in lace.

"Eternal regrets": the words reappear from tomb to tomb, stamped on marble, engraved in stone, set among multicolored ceramic flowers, or prettily traced on the black-bordered white enamel hearts of earlier days. You, the forever dead—the living regret you in black-and-white and in color, and they've written down their regrets one last time; but for what kind of eternity? The living weep over you, and their tears turn hard as these sealed stones, they rust away with the iron fences of your enclosures and wither with the chrysanthemums. Do they ever think of the regrets heaped underground with your remains? Do they ever hear you chanting litanies of regrets for your lost dreams, your heartaches, your wasted efforts, your failed lives? A hymn of despair, trailing in the night wind . . . "Eternal regrets." And also: "Time passes, memories remain."

I enjoy speaking courteously to those unknown dead, all beautiful now as they meet and mingle under their cloak of earth. I have no fear of their ashes, their roots, their composted nails and braids, their wasted rags, their skeletons still stippled with flesh or perfectly smooth, cleaned and polished by subterranean time, or their bony architectures (vaults, nodes, caverns, whitened ledges, sunken cathedrals), not even the empty sockets of their eyes and their vermin. They are there, and that's all. I don't think with horror that I too shall be a body destroyed and consumed; nor, poetically, that I shall no longer be a body at all but ashes to nourish the earth, with starry grasses springing from my brow. I simply don't think about it. They're below ground, I'm above; they're darkness, I'm daylight; they sleep when I lie sleepless; they have forgotten what they were searching for, which is what I'm searching for too, sure of not knowing any more about it than they. They're there beneath my feet, they no longer hear me, their skulls are hollow as bubbles, and they couldn't care less. Go on sleeping, beautiful dead ones: we keep our vigils in a dream and shed our tears for pictures.

I often took her to cemeteries. We had our dead to visit, and we didn't wait for their flowers to crumble. Since they were scattered over France, we couldn't pay our respects to all of them. We'd go to the nearest one and ask him to convey to the others a share of our thoughts, a few petals from our flowers. Of late these outings had been real expeditions, but she had no desire to give them up. They were the only ones she allowed herself, and she garnered all her strength for them.

After parking the car as near her front door as possible, I used to find her waiting for me sitting upright in her chair, made up, hair in place, a mauve hat on her head. A necklace of delicate pearls stood out against her black collar. She had put on her four rings and, on her wrist, a heavy gold bracelet that she would coquettishly shake so that it jangled against the crook of her cane—a sign that she was feeling well and that I should refrain from making comments. The room was fragrant with Cinq de Molyneux. On her knees lay a handkerchief with which she would pretend to wipe away a tear, before ceremoniously handing it to me to slip into her coat pocket. She had given her head, grave and powdered, the look of an antique tragic mask. I felt like a member of some sacred cult, but also like a mourner hired for the occasion. To tell the truth, I felt a nervous impulse to burst out laughing, but there was no question of giving in to it. She would have taken it very badly; she was already becoming irritated with Juliette, who as she helped her on with her coat and gloves was getting tangled in the lining of the sleeves or putting the right-hand forefinger where the thumb should be. We helped her walk to the door. She gave herself a nasty look in the hall mirror, raising her eyebrows, hiding the cane behind her back, full of scorn for this clumsy woman stuffed into an overcoat and incapable of the slightest initiative.

We would settle her in the car as best we could. She tried to look around her in a calm and dignified manner, but the outside noise and bustle must have set her head spinning, and her efforts to master her giddiness showed in her clenched teeth, in the cane clutched tight against her breast the way stone saints in churches clasp their crucifixes.

On the way, as she became accustomed to the changing scenery, she would relax. From time to time, to recover her strength, she would shut her eyes behind her gloved hand and ask me for the tenth time if I hadn't forgotten the flowers.

We had special permission from the town hall to take our car into the vast suburban graveyard. It was surrounded by the ugliest high-rises imaginable, checkered with laundry hung out to dry at every window. Each time we drove through the entrance, she deplored the dreariness of these expanses without fir trees or cypresses or soul. We stopped at the desired row, marked by an all-white tomb on top of which a marble book, streaking with time, lay open to the words "To our beloved child" beneath a pretty little angel at its prayers. Pushing and pulling, I would guide her among the tombs until we came to our very own. There, standing on unsteady legs in a semblance of balance, she would strike the granite with the tip of her cane, as if to say, "Are you there, my dead ones?" At that moment it scarcely mattered who in particular lay beneath the stone.

While I arranged the flowers, she spoke to them in a low voice. A tear—an invariable tear—slipped from her left eye. Hooking her cane on the button fastened just below the collar of her coat, she took out her handkerchief for a moment, sniffling as she put it back in her pocket. Then she took up her cane and again struck the stone—the signal for departure.

Hanging on my arm, she would lumber into motion, poking furiously with her cane at vases of shriveled chrysanthemums, shrugging her shoulder, finally coming to a stop. At this point I was supposed to look into her eyes and take her hands in mine; and I was allowed to laugh. Her face would turn pink—she herself would break into silent laughter, shaking her head and saying, "Just look at the two of us!" We would stumble the rest of our way to the car, greeting as we went all the deceased in the central avenue. "We're not being serious," she'd say, "but after all, you can't spend your whole life crying."

Yes, autumn has been lovely this year. Hardly enough wind to trouble the plump, rough chrysanthemum heads, and no rain at all. On All Saints' Day, the living in their Sunday best throng festive graveyards; monumental traffic jams block the entrances; entire families arrive to enjoy the sun. On the Day of the Dead there are no burials. I have no one to bury, in any case. I'm going to the hospital to see my sleeping lady.

She's holding her own. She withstands all treatments. I saw the head doctor again. He seemed angry. "It's amazing," he said. "With the doses we're giving her, she *has* to wake up." "What can you expect," I replied, "she doesn't *want* to." He had difficulty hiding the contemptuous pity he felt for me; he turned his back. Since then he's avoided me.

As soon as I reach her section, it's become a ritual, I start looking around for the chief nurse—a slender blonde woman, still young, with gentle eyes of periwinkle blue. She catches sight of me, gives me a little smile as she shakes her head, and holding out her hand to me, says, "No change."

I await this moment with beating heart. What will I do on the day when she triumphantly tells me, "Hurry, she's woken up!" That is, without any doubt, the pleasure she would like to offer me. I tremble at the thought. To this kind woman I don't dare confess my dread: that her sleep will end. The dread of opening the door and seeing her look at me with her faded eyes and reproach me for everything. Am I afraid of seeing her come back to life? Is it so inadmissible that day after day I wander without a murmur down these corridors, submitting to the omnipotent hospital routine without ever rebelling against her distinguished saviors? What is it they want to save? That's not their problem. The heart goes on beating—just listen to the beat of this robust heart, this indomitable machine, and trust in our powers. And what if I tell you that each contraction of that beating heart sends a wild surge of blood to overwhelm her foundering brain and drown it a little deeper? Come, come: we'll find one small cell still functioning that can reopen the stubbornly shut eye and convince your incredulity that the medical profession has done its duty. No! She won't obey you. She isn't going to see you gathered at her bedside to torment her; and she won't see me perched on her bed stroking her bare shoulders and her limp hands swollen with edema, or replacing faded flowers with fresh ones. What they want is this: to have her go under slowly, little by little, so that afterward they can say with reassuring satisfaction, "We did everything we could."

In her room a new sight awaits me. It's not the first time she's been fed through a tube, but I've never yet been present at a "meal." A nurse is standing near the bed among a whole apparatus of wires, tubes, and various receptacles. From now on, they've decided, this arrangement will be permanent. "It makes for easier handling," the nurse tells me. She is holding a bowl filled with mush and a wooden pestle. She stuffs the thick mixture into a large funnel set on steel stand. From the tip of the funnel a siphon leads, in a series of twists, to the tube that penetrates her nostril. At each prod of the pestle, mush drips down to her stomach with a soft rubbery sound.

"It's horrible. You've got to stop."

Unflustered, the little nurse smiles at me: "If it makes you uncomfortable, you don't have to stay. The amount is compulsory."

Then, changing her mind (as if she thought: what do I care, you manage with your comatose old woman), she pours the rest of the mush into the funnel (it almost overflows), drops the pestle into it, where it slowly settles, and leaves.

I move closer to the bed. Noisy breathing; sunken eyes; damp forehead; matted hair; over the cheekbones, gray skin. And they stuff her with mush! At the foot of the bed, a blue line zigzags across the fever chart, the list of drugs is longer, I read "urea" and "diabetes," I look at her, her breast rising and falling under the sheet. How can you manage to still be here? Is the path so long to where you're going? Can't you glimpse that iridescent sky? What kind of requiem are they singing? And if they're calling you, why are you resisting so hard? If you come back, I won't be able to help you—you'll be like a water plant stagnating in a greenish pond, choked with growths, a decomposing vegetable existence.

I mentally pinch myself—it's crazy talking to her like this. What if she heard me? I bend down and brush her forehead with a kiss; then run away. I'd thought I'd seen a tear twinkling at the corner of her eye, under the lashes. I hurry down the corridor. Periwinkle stops me. She looks worried.

"The doctor asked me to talk to you. If nothing changes in the next couple of days, we'll have to make a decision."

"Oh? What kind of decision? You're not going to kill her?"

"What a horrible thing to say! You must be tired. Honestly!" (She really has very pretty eyes.) "You must understand. Her coma's not deep, but in spite of very strong medication, she hasn't woken up. That's not normal. We might need to consider a minor operation."

"They wouldn't dare—"

"Don't get excited. All right." She takes me by the arm, and we walk together toward the elevator. She's very gentle, she talks to me as if I was a lunatic. "Don't get excited. It won't amount to anything."

"Nothing at all. Just cutting open her skull to 'see what's going on.' Is that it? It's out of the question. I'm categorically against it. They have no right to poke around in her brain. To find what—a solution to the puzzle? I won't hear of it."

Once again I see the funnel and the mush, and for the space of a second I remember that my medicine chest is filled with tranquilizers and sleeping pills. Would I have the nerve?

Periwinkle is gazing at me disconsolately. "In that case, I don't think Dr. Z can keep her here much longer."

"I see. It's blackmail. This is where people are revived—and if they don't revive, they're thrown out. Excuse me—transferred."

I don't hear her reply. I think how kind they are to inform me of their plans, but that in any case they won't take my reluctance into consideration. The day she was admitted I had to sign the usual form, which stipulated that "Dr. Z is authorized to perform any emergency operation on the patient if clearly necessary," and so forth. I see her sleeping face, the lusterless hair on the pillow, and the glint of a tear. I grab Periwinkle's arm.

"Tell me something. Can she hear?"

Her face lights up. I can see she'd like to cheer me up.

"Why, of course, it's perfectly possible. We've had people come out of comas that lasted for weeks and repeat everything they heard. Don't be discouraged!"

I see . . . The elevator still hasn't arrived. I'll run down the three flights of tiled stairs. In a few days, Periwinkle will be holding me in her arms. A garbage can must have tipped over in the stairway. I pass soiled bandages and bits of bloody cotton. I want to throw up.

Three days later, nothing has changed. Rain is falling on Paris and on the hospital. Gusts are carrying away the last leaves. November is taking over. It's noon. The bearded doctor has summoned me, he'll see me at the end of his rounds. He has to talk to me—no doubt a decision needs to be made.

I pass through the entrance, drive to the far end of the dripping grounds and pull up under the last plane tree. It's time. I hop my way between puddles to the door of the wing, then proceed upstairs amid the racket of lunch wagons and the persistent smells of boiled vegetables, ham and mashed potatoes, and stewed fruit. The gang of white coats has finished its tour and is talking things over in a circle at the head of the corridor. When he notices me, the bearded man leaves the group and approaches with one hand outstretched, friendly but grave. He leads me into the glass cage where files, charts, and reports are classified and which he uses as his office. So we'll talk.

"I'll sum up the situation for you as of today," he begins. "A cerebral hemorrhage in the right side of the brain has caused a paralysis of the left half of the body and brought on a coma. The coma isn't deep—the EEG isn't flat. Do you understand?"

"I understand, but I would like to tell you about her."

"Still, the coma has lasted more than three weeks. There have been a few minor incidents, but essentially the patient's condition is stable. At this point we feel that, therapeutically speaking, we've tried everything we could to bring her out of the coma. We can't stop now. We've got to try something else. Are you following me?"

"I'm following you, but I would like to tell you something about her."

"The latest tests point to a new factor. That is, we're now almost positive that it wasn't a ruptured blood vessel that caused the hemorrhage. I've been in touch several times with your family doctor. He'd had lab tests done that showed a rise in her sedimentation rate. Do you remember that?"

"I do remember, but let me tell you about her."

"For three weeks now the rate has continued to rise. So it's very possible that the formation of a tumor was at the origin of the stroke. We've got to be sure about that. We've got to operate."

"Listen to me. You don't know her. You don't know what she was like before. She had already declined considerably, you see. What do you expect to salvage? Left side, right side, it's all gone under. She couldn't take it anymore. If she went to sleep, it's because she was tired of struggling. Leave her alone."

I'm pathetic. I'm beneath contempt. I hardly know what I'm saying. My arguments are so much air—have I lost my power to defend her? In any case, he's not even listening. All my energy has deserted me. I've become a victim of the irresistible process to which I committed her and which nothing now can stop. He sees me weakening. Sure of his authority, he pushes me a little deeper into despair.

"I've made a point of talking to you about this. I could perfectly well not have done so. You put us in charge of the patient. It's our duty to do all we can to save her—which in this case means bringing her back to consciousness."

"And salvage whatever is to be salvaged."

"In a manner of speaking."

"And afterward?"

"That's a premature question."

"In any case, she'll stay in your unit."

"As long as there's anything we can do for her, she will."

"And after that?"

He shrugs his shoulders; he wants to leave. I stop him: "In your opinion, is she strong enough for an operation?"

"For the time being she is. We mustn't wait too long. We're giving ourselves forty-eight hours to prepare her for it. Excuse me, I have to go."

What could be more reasonable than that? Or more humane? One can only accept. That's all there is to it.

The corridors have emptied: lunch break. I set off toward her room and as I approach it, a sense of muffled shame comes over me. I've given my consent. Each day I've abandoned her a little more; now I'm sending her to the slaughterhouse. For the first time I wish I could open the door and see her looking at me, smiling, stretching out her hand to me. But she's asleep, openmouthed, her feeding tube inside one nostril, her two forearms connected to bottles filled with transparent liquid diminishing drop by drop. Underneath the bed is the jar at the end of the urinary catheter. She's a machine that breathes in and out and refuses to stop. This is the body they want to operate on, the skull they want to open. Like an engine dismantled to locate the defective part.

I notice her hair and suddenly realize they'll have to shave her. No, no, I'm not playing along anymore. I go out into the corridor to find the bearded man and tell him that I've changed my mind, that I won't let them touch a hair on her head. No one's there except Periwinkle, taking small steps as she approaches, her cheeks pink—she's just had lunch, she must have drunk her espresso and smoked a cigarette. I catch her as she goes by and take her into the room.

"Just the person I was looking for," she says.

I pull her to the foot of the bed.

"Look at her," I tell her. "She was a beautiful woman."

"I can believe that. She's not so bad now, you know."

"She was beautiful. Her hair was silver and her eyes were green. She hated the idea of growing old and ugly. And now—if she opened her eyes, I wouldn't dare pass her a mirror. In two days they operate—"

"Maybe it's for the best!" Her mauve eyes stare straight into mine; she lays her hand on my hand as it clutches the metal bar. "You understand," she says, and I see her eyes become misty.

I do understand. She's right. I give her a quick kiss. She's not surprised. I slip into my coat. She takes a twice-folded tan envelope from the pocket of her smock.

"I'm sorry about the wrapping and having to give it to you like this. It's just—you've noticed how swollen her fingers are. We were obliged to remove her rings. They had to cut them, naturally. Here they are."

She hands me the little package. I stuff it in my handbag, thank her, and flee.

In the hollow of my hand, two shattered rings. I turn them over; I warm them; if I shut my hand tight, they hurt. Two golden rings that never left you. The link that made your life what it was is broken: passion, attachment, submission, commitment. The best, the worst, and the rest.

In a white room, a stranger's hand took your warm, inert hand and with an adroit strip of his pincers severed forty years of marriage.

I remember another white room: a cold room, another person's sleep, a stranger's hand slipping into mine a ring like one of these. He said: "We removed it—we thought you might like to keep it." The ring burned my palm. My head was spinning as I restored it to the thin, brittle finger of a stony hand that was clutching emptiness.

To each his own way . . . The two of you never had your golden wedding anniversary. You never grew old together, gently cradled in rediscovered tenderness. You never rested at one another's side, never gazed into one another's face in the calm recess of a shared old age. "Will he ever stop?" you asked wearily. For him, growing old did not exist; it was an accident that only happened to others. He was spared the awareness of his error, he left without knowing what he had become, and you stayed on alone with your dream of retirement in a warm land. I can still remember how you longed for an ordinary life: you would have liked to be a serene old lady, sitting in the shade of lindens in front of the family house, watching your grandchildren scampering across the meadow. You would have enjoyed opening old cupboards, slipping lavender sachets between white sheets, simmering big copper pots full of red jam, and Sundays, after Mass at the village church, strolling along the paths of your garden counting the rosebushes in flower, your steps slow, your arm resting on that of a man whom the years would have chastened.

You were never to enjoy that tenderness—walking together and speaking of the past with misted eyes, stopping now and then to yank out a tuft of weed, even consoling one another for old crises simply because time has passed (for good or for ill) and most of all because there are two people close to one another, warming one another under the April sun, strolling among the acacias, making plans for the coming evening or for the following morning. You would only have an involuntary, lonely retirement, with a busy street below and, beyond the windowpane, an idle sparrow hopping between three potted geraniums.

The rings are shattered; you will leave the world with bare hands. You are now more alone than ever, stripped each day of the emblems of your life.

I won't keep anything. There will be no museum. I won't fill up cupboards or accumulate cardboard boxes in attics where memories molder.

Returning to her place, I touch with eyes and hands objects that still speak of her forcefully—the cane leaning against the chair, colored yarn spilling out of the workbasket, the embroidery frame still hanging on the armrest. On the back of the chair, the lace where she rested her head.

The seated woman is no longer waiting for me. The scene is out of date.

Juliette in her anxiety paces from room to room. She feels useless. She cannot bear the clothes in the closet, the make-up in the bathroom, the shoes by the bed, the eyeglasses. She tells me: "We ought to straighten things up and get ready. Why don't they bring her back here? It's better to die in your own bed." Like an animal sensing an approaching storm, she can't keep still. She keeps saying, "This time, you know, this time it won't last long." She wants her dead lady home, so that she can dress her, adorn her with perfume and gems, and mourn her between two candles. She wants a fine death, not the hospital morgue. I let her say what she wants, I don't know any more, I don't want anything. I no longer see her, she's too far away, she's disappeared from my heaven, the sleepwalker no longer strides from peak to peak. She is buried in dense foliage and I can no longer hear her singing.

In the room, everything is still. A few rays of pale sunlight light up the dust on the closed piano. How could she contemplate all day long a piano that was no longer tuned and that she never opened, knowing she wouldn't dare touch the keys with only one hand? Higher up, framed against the wall, her familiar dead look down on me sedately. I imagine them standing in line on a cloud, waiting for their traveler. I smile stupidly at the thought. I remember Kienholz's seated lady with, at her back, the portrait of her hero looking down on her timeless expectancy. No aging widow lives without a conspicuously placed picture of the man who was the first to leave.

These men sometimes sport mustaches. You find their portraits above the piano, or between two china vases, or on the lace covering of a bedside table. Most often they are shown in the prime of life, their firm jaws emphasized by a white collar or a sober cravat. Not uncommonly, a gold chain or watch will highlight the distinction of their dress. Their gazes steady, occasionally overbearing, only rarely tinged with melancholy, they gravely and pointlessly contemplate from the depths of their cardboard nothingness the world they left behind them on a day like any other. They may have been in pain or unaware, sorrowful or serene, knowing in any case that they had fulfilled their duty or their destiny—in short, that they had lived. Now we cry over them, we celebrate them, we deck them with flowers, we go on loving these dear departed, we do not forget them, and with untroubled eyes they observe the quiet, boring lives of their widows. They had often made them wait, cry, suffer, and be misled, and only rarely laugh. Frequently they made war, money, children, and other women, too. We no longer blame them—we revere them. We sometimes love them better dead than alive, our dear departed. Their images fade only gradually, along with their widows' failing sight and declining days. These men are legion and all alike, sharing the privilege of having been the first to go. Death, that leveler of memories, has given them a sheen dear to widows' hearts that extends like a saving shroud over all the monuments erected to their memory.

She had been a widow for ten years. She became one by surprise at a time when, ill as she already was, it had been her life we worried about every day. But it was he who went, without warning—the invulnerable hero, the man of her life.

I remember that when he died, in January, Paris was covered with snow. The day after Christmas I took him to a clinic on Boulevard Arago, a stone's throw from the Lion of Belfort. Pain had made him surly. He couldn't stand the anguished looks she cast him as she sat huddled in her chair in the farthest corner of the living room, leaving him room to walk back and forth, hunched over, smoking one cigarette after another. He couldn't stand her questions—"Are you feeling better? Does it hurt a little less?"—or the advice she proffered in a small, fearful voice: "You should lie down. You shouldn't smoke so much." He could stand her tears even less. He scarcely said good-bye to her. I can still see him slamming the door behind him, crossing the sidewalk bareheaded, his coat thrown over his shoulders, refusing to lean on my arm, furious that he had to ride in an ambulance. He scowled as he climbed into the front seat.

He didn't even glance at the window where, her forehead pressed against the pane, she was shyly waving to him.

A white, snow-covered clinic; a white room; hypodermics, disinfectants; an operation; pain, soon followed by morphine; absolute, wordless silence. And I, on New Year's Day, standing petrified at the foot of the bed, with my bouquet of holly hidden behind me, I found myself wishing happy New Year to a corpse.

She never saw him sink into his last sleep; she never saw him at all. It was too cold. She wasn't allowed out. She remained seated in her chair while he journeyed to the frozen soil of his native village. She was never told that under the north wind and the frozen grass the ground was so hard that the dead were no longer buried. The morgues were full up. He had to wait for the next thaw in an out-of-the-way corner of the little church before reaching his burial place. Around the altar and outside the church door, the flowers of the funeral wreaths shattered like glass.

Her acceptance of his death was staggering. He'd abandoned her so often that this may have seemed to her like one more separation. I never saw her cry much. She looked elegant in mourning, which changed nothing in her appearance since she had favored mauve and purple for a long time.

There were several months of real euphoria. A mania overcame her for tidying things up. She reread and classified all her letters, keeping only a small selection, burning all the rest without batting an eyelid. She would stand leaning on her cane in the middle of the apartment and instruct Juliette to move a piece of furniture, or take down a picture, scolding her for her slowness. She was now captain of the ship. No man would ever again make her keep quiet, or cry, or pine. She was collecting her strength. Would she have time to live out her widowhood in peace?

That summer—she was still relatively agile—we made a brief pilgrimage to the Alsace of her origins. She showed me the house where she was born, her ivy-mantled lycée, her mother's tomb, and the town hall and church where she had said yes. She told me the story of her childhood and youth. She wanted to pick up the thread of that particular past, as if her newfound widow's solitude had freed a nostalgic individual within her whom a life lived for and around one man had buried in the depths of her memory.

On our way back, we made a detour through another countryside—the one where he lay underground—and spoke a few flower-sweetened words to him. She was very calm; distant, too, facing this massive tomb she disliked, no doubt thinking with melancholy that some day she would lie next to him and that, in any event, none of this would matter in the least.

What was now left of her love story? While with an air of resignation she gently prodded the marble with her cane, I felt that the only thing that might provide an answer was her enigmatic smile: a smile that she seemed to let fade over the gilt lettering of the freshly carved name as she said, before turning away, "Good-bye, poor darling." She would never have dared show pity for him while he was alive. He was dead; she no longer feared him; and she forgave him everything.

She would return home and never go out again, settling into a solitude that, she hoped, would quietly coast until it reached its term, in calm waters, if that were possible. She would keep herself as busy as her strength permitted, taking care that her face not become her antagonist in an old age threatened by paralysis; and she would pray heaven to spare her the degradation of still greater infirmity.

It was too late to try and understand, too late to analyze how successive solitudes had distorted her needs and hobbled her freedom as a woman; in a word, it was too late to look back. She would return to a house as over-furnished as her past was cluttered with sorrows. She would put up a portrait of the dear departed over the piano and each week decorate it with a bouquet of garnet-red carnations, the flowers he used to give her on each of their wedding anniversaries. She would sit down in her chair as if on the last stone by a pathway, sorting her memories and saving a few as ex-votos and memorial plaques, and then she would wait in her graveyard for nothing more to happen at all.

Three days passed, then four and five, and I've stopped counting. Periwinkle has gone off on vacation. "A long one?" I asked her. "No, I'll be seeing you again." That was all she would tell me before she slipped way, her high heels clattering over the floor. Eventually she turned around and gave me a smile (sweet, no doubt, but distant). I'm angry at her for leaving me. I didn't dare tell her I'd miss her.

She turned me over to a squad of new nurses. They shrug their shoulders when I question them, not nastily, but as if to say, "You think they tell us anything? We just perform. We glide around corridors, we hustle around answering bells, we open doors and close them, we bathe people, we I.V., we thermometer, and leave, and when we come back there's a different face on the pillow. How can we worry about what's happening to people? We haven't the time, that's the way it is."

What are they waiting for? I didn't go after them—they were the ones who talked about operating. Since then, nothing in the white room has changed. There's no one to explain. The intern is hiding; the bearded man has become invisible. Can they be avoiding me? What kind of a surprise are they planning for me? Two or three times a day I lie in wait in order to foil their secret plans. But it's always the same; things seem to have settled into a vast unchanging rhythm of hospital clockwork. Routine has taken over, slowly revolving its notched gears and describing a circle from which I no longer emerge: a circle of white walls, ether, and formalin with, at its center, a heart that beats and keeps beating, toward which my steps, now part of the rhythm, constantly turn.

Characterless days are passing, freighted with autumn and a sorrow I can't define. Am I sad, gloomy, discouraged, prostrate? Or am I resigned, weary, just carried along? Am I sad, gloomy . . . ? I can't tell. I keep moving, I link a new day to each day that's done, day after day. I keep moving like a dreamer through other people's reality, as though there were no tangible part of me that could still communicate with the living or share their gestures, rituals, and habits. I watch others hurrying down the street, going into stores, and coming out burdened with packages, getting into their cars, strolling arm in arm on the sidewalk, stopping, conversing, moving on. I watch them all conscientiously keeping busy, living their honest lives as passersby, pedestrians, ants. And I make my own way in their midst, my footsteps and my urgency mingle in the dust they raise; but I can't see myself hurrying, or walking along the curb, or going into a store. I've lost touch.

I float through the city asleep and only wake up at the hospital entrance, and there the circle of walls, ether, and formalin closes around me. My schedule comes to life, I see it unwind like a streamer between the entrance and the building at the far end of the grounds. I note the time and the weather, I'm sure what day, month, and year it is. Today is Saturday—five weeks soon. Five weeks of coma, absence, drift, and sleep: both a lot and a little (so very little) in a lifetime.

Today, making my way across town, I feel that something has changed. My brain at last wakes up to what it is in a moment of inattention, as I blindly pass from one neighborhood to the next. There it is, inscribed in shining letters that blink on the bare branches of plane trees: "Christmas." Christmas is coming, and in the streets this morning the first wreaths appeared, and trees decorated with silver balls that bob in December wind. Why do they have to celebrate everything? We've barely emerged from the graveyard chrysanthemums, and now we'll have to fight our way through fir trees, holly, and mistletoe. What is the obsessive anxiety that makes people cling to dates and name days and birthdays? And then prettify them with ribbons and wreaths? I wish Christmas would wait and not disturb our routine, not assault us with its endless succession of chocolates, toys, and glowing smiles.

She used to love Christmas. She began enjoying it weeks ahead of time: it was her holiday and ritual, her yearning for Alsace and its forests of fir trees. Earlier—long ago—December for us meant expectation and excitement: paper being crumpled behind a door we were forbidden to open; smells of candles, pastry, and lemon; golden-brown cakes enclosed in tall metal boxes that were hidden under dishtowels on the top shelves of closets; ribbons or favors or strands of tinsel spilled along the fringe of a rug. Every day brought a new smell or sound (a sleigh bell tinkling at the far end of the apartment, a muted "Silent Night" on the Victrola), any trace of the celebration being prepared made us thrill with emotion until that glittering night when all secrets would be revealed. Later, her immobility never kept her from planning her mysteries. I would come into the living room and find her (apparently for her own sake) concealing some piece of work or other under the cloth cover of her basket. She sewed and embroidered innumerable doilies, handkerchiefs, and napkin rings that Juliette would help her wrap in brightly colored paper. A good part of her dismal winters was enlivened with these preparations. On December 24 I'd bring her a Christmas tree, and from the top of the Alsatian sideboard we would take down the old cartons where ever since her childhood she had preserved glass balls, flaking or transparent, squashed cotton angels, and little painted wooden figures "Made in Germany." I would transform the tree into an outmoded shrine as I decorated it, following the orders she issued with the tip of her cane, looking very serious, shutting one eye or cocking her head to evaluate the results.

Today is Saturday. December has begun. The air in Paris is by no means cold. How I wish that Christmas would stop hovering on the horizon of this dark declining year! I imagine myself taking the elevator with my little tree in my arms, getting off at her floor amid the obstreperous sounds of television, and making my way to her room under the curious eyes of the other patients. No. Christmas in the hospital? I couldn't do it.

As I reach my floor, I wonder if Periwinkle is back. I'm feeling lost and need her company. I walk on without seeing anyone until as I enter the corridor I'm suddenly grabbed by the intern, who's trussed up in a long white apron. Why is he taking me by the arm? Why the rush? What's happening?

"I'm coming with you," he says. "You'll see, things are getting better."

I stop, rooted to the spot. What did he say?

"Yes, things are getting better, you'll see. A definite improvement since this morning."

What am I about to find? What have they done to her? What is it he's going to show me?

"You see? You should never give up hope. We told you her coma wasn't deep."

He's overjoyed; I've turned to ice. Streets in their Christmas decorations flash through my mind, we're entering the room, flooded with light. Two white shapes are leaning over the bed. I can hear their saccharine, singsong voices, as though they were talking to a baby or a halfwit. "Feeling better, aren't we, Madame? We're going to wake up now, aren't we? Yes, we're going to wake up . . ."

Where is Periwinkle? I stagger as I approach: two women I don't know spewing baby talk, addressing this pathetic body that I watch rise and fall with its gasping, raucous breathing.

"You call this improvement?"

"Of course! Now I want you to look and listen."

Perfectly sure of himself, he motions the nurses to the foot of the bed, where they stare at me. He's going to show me what he can do. I feel sick as I wait for the conjuror to wave his magic wand and . . . and what? Bring her out of her trance? He slaps her, pulls her hair, pinches her arm and shoulder. "Madame, do you hear me? Madame!"

I hear a muffled groan painfully emerging from the gauze-covered orifice. I look at the face streaked with sweat, the cheekbones spotted as if with yesterday's rouge, and the eyelids—the eyelids have risen a fraction of an inch, and they remain there as she moans again, a deep, drawn-out, unbearable moan. He's about to repeat his act when I grab his wrist and sink my nails into it. Dumbfounded, he angrily frees himself and gives me a baleful look.

"Make up your mind what you want."

"Get the hell out of here!"

He is about to reply, then changes his mind, scornfully shrugging his shoulders (he's decided that I'm unbalanced), and strides out of the room with the nurses at his heels.

I collapse on the chair by the bed. I rest my forehead on her swollen hand, where the rings have left furrows in the gray flesh.

The skin is warm. You're alive, you're still there, underneath your husk. Can you see me? Can you hear me? Is that possible? How deep are the pools in which sleepwalkers sleep? Have you decided to emerge from your dream and float to the surface? I glimpsed the muddied green of your eyes a few moments ago; now they've vanished. What happened to your transparency and your lightness? What and whom are you coming back for? I whisper to you now, I've stopped calling you back, I like you better asleep, can't you understand? I can't offer you any fuller life than an iris's in the garden. Don't come back, don't prevaricate, make yourself a cradle of water lilies and forget about us. So many of your capillaries have already drowned there are very few left to salvage. Listen to those siren voices, follow them without regret—after all, between these four walls they're not offering you music or a requiem but jolts, noises, and sounds that hurt. Go away, my sweet one. I'll cover your escape. Here, the time for living is over.

I feel a hand on my shoulder and turn around. Periwinkle is smiling at me. I take her slender hand in mine and restrain my impulse to press it to my lips. There she is. That's nice. That's better. I won't be alone anymore.

"Hello," she says, "Were you talking to her?"

"Yes. I was asking her to go away."

"You know"—she hesitates—"she can hear you."

"I don't believe it. What about you—do you think she's any better?"

"She's less remote. Her sensitivity has increased."

"She can groan to show she's in pain, that's all. A triumph of medicine after five weeks of coma! Bravo."

Periwinkle sighs. She is still standing behind me. One hand rests on my shoulder; with the other she pushes aside a mass of my straight hair, a curtain that I often hide behind. Her voice is muted.

"Look at her eyes. They're halfway open. And they aren't so glassy."

I look. Teary lids barely disclose the rims of muddy-green irises.

"Those aren't her eyes I see—they belong to somebody half dead, somebody being brought back to life no matter what."

"You can't blame us for—"

Her gentleness suddenly gets on my nerves: I shake her off. She walks away, leans against a wall, and looks at me sadly.

"I don't blame you for anything. Not you. But don't expect me to be consoled by phrases that sound memorized. You're the only person here I can talk to. The only one who seems to listen. The only one I can tell how fed up I am with this circus and that the one thing I want for her is to die."

"Hush! Not so loud. She can hear you."

"So let her hear me."

The face is motionless. I wait for a tear or a sign that will make me die of shame. Nothing. Everything is very quiet. A fly beats against the pane—how has it survived in this air reeking of disinfectant? In the distance, a faint rumble of traffic. (She's better? They're crazy!)

I get up and start to leave. Periwinkle watches me putting on my coat.

"Come back this afternoon. It'll be better. Dr. Z will be here."

"Don't worry, I'll be here. If everything's okay, just put her in a wheelchair and wait for me outside the elevator. That way will be a nice surprise."

A woebegone Periwinkle extends a hand that I don't touch.

I'm back at the hospital by three. The bearded man nabs me in the corridor. He rubs his hands. He seems very pleased.

"They told you things are better? If she keeps making progress, she'll be able to leave the unit in a few days."

"Running all the way . . . To go where?"

"You should get busy finding a room in a general practice ward. That won't be easy here. Perhaps in a private clinic. But the best of all would be to take her home."

"What do you mean? What kind of shape will she be in?"

"You can't expect a miracle. She'll be bedridden. And of course, in a state of dementia. But as far as we're concerned, we're through."

"In other words, you're giving me a choice between an asylum and a nightmare."

"Come on, you're exaggerating."

"Do you honestly feels she's been 'revived'?"

"It won't be long now. Don't give up. Keep checking in. The worst is over. See you soon."

Periwinkle was present at the end of the conversation. She's looking at me. I see her through a haze.

"Tell me I'm dreaming."

"Don't panic. They're very optimistic. But for the time being she can't be moved. I'm not supposed to tell you that, so keep it to yourself."

"They're really that eager to get rid of her."

"It's not always easy—"

"I know, I know." Several seconds, several very long seconds, a minute, perhaps two minutes pass. Our eyes meet, shy away, turn back, again diverge. Sighs, hesitations—what do we do now, what do we say? Stay, leave, laugh, cry? I offer her a cigarette.

"You know we don't smoke here."

"Of course . . . He said 'in a state of dementia.' Is that a common expression here?"

"You mustn't let words frighten you. We use the term 'dementia praecox' or 'senile dementia.'"

"In her case, what does it mean? That she's crazy?"

"Certainly not." She hesitates, gazing at the floor, and smiles at me. "It's a word that refers to the gradual deterioration of certain psychological functions—"

"In other words, she can regain the appearances of life, but not her sanity."

"Yes and no—it's actually impossible to say. It all depends on her physical stamina. Her heart is sound. She can keep going for days, or weeks—months, even. You can't tell." She looks down again. "My father lasted two years like that. It was very hard, but 'what can you do,' after all?"

"Your father? I see . . . Did he speak to you? Did he recognize you?"

"Never. One morning we found him dead."

"A rotting plant that can still moan and feel pain without knowing why. They're crazy."

Periwinkle smiles at me out of her mauve eyes.
"You don't want to see her again?"
"No. I don't want to see her anymore. I'm scared."

To stop talking, stop writing, stop thinking!

Words are useless scales that slither down my skin and fall along my path, like tears of ice reverberating in the depths of a cellar.

Struggling with metallic darkness, moving along a marble corridor, running headlong down the steps of an endless winding stair . . . Weeping haphazardly, spilling disordered words that bounce down those steps to disappear in the dark corners of the landings. That was me.

I'd like to stop. I can't. So I let myself go.

The story continues. Dum de dum, repeating itself in my ears. It isn't a symphony, it isn't an opera. A few pungent notes: the beginning of the Chopin waltz she sometimes played in the evening. No way of remembering the waltz's name. Dum de dum. But it wouldn't mean anything to you. You'd have to hear it.

Dum de dum—another memory to trip over as I hurtle down the stair. So I'll never get to the end of this story. Chopin's waltz is tripping through my head. Dum de dum . . . She'd be tired when she came home at night. She'd walk across the apartment, with a cup of coffee in one hand and her cigarette holder between her lips, lithe and humming as she went, gliding though the narrow room as if it were a stage. She used to sit down, open the fallboard after wiping it with her sleeve, set her cup on the wooden rectangle by the keys, and, closing one eye to ward off the smoke of her cigarette, begin the waltz. Dum de dum. Haltingly at first, then letting it run, easily, flowingly accompanying the tune with a faint murmur of her low voice, as if she were hearing a secret she did not wish to share. I would be hanging at her fingertips, abruptly enchanted by this rare moment of tranquility. She would stop. More, please! But she would shake her head wearily, her eyes shut, then pick up her cold coffee, close the piano, and stand up, miles away.

(I can no longer hear a sonata, a heady waltz, or a nocturne without confronting her ghost and her rippling notes scattered through the dark of empty houses, fragments hovering on the brink of sorrow—two chords for a sigh, three bars for a regret. And then the shutting of a fallboard.)

A piano lies in wait for me on the landing, two pianos, ten pianos. The stair I'm endlessly hurtling down is a gigantic keyboard, each step a key that I hammer with my stride. I'm running in time to a waltz—dum de dum—it won't stop, it keeps leading me on toward the place where I'll find her. Will you come back, poor shadow, will you rise to me out of the mist and play your waltz once again?

I wish they'd let me sleep; a sleep without any chance encounters. But if I close my eyes, images accost me. Now a sleepwalker myself, I run along the edge of night hoping to forget them, but they dog my steps.

I'm walking down a cobbled village street. It's the morning hour when housewives do their errands, moving along the sidewalk or pausing outside a shop window, a basket in one hand, turning around to watch me pass. I'm pushing a wheelchair equipped with high-spoked wheels like old nineteenth-century bikes. The wheelchair bumps over the cobblestones, jarring its occupant, who does not complain. Her hands, in white kid gloves, hang onto the armrests, and she simply murmurs, "Not so fast, not so fast." But I don't hear her. Nearby a dog is barking. I have the feeling that I've been walking for hours, I wish this strange journey would end, but I don't recognize the street, and I can no longer find the door of the house where I was meant to arrive. I don't, in fact, know where I'm going. But I keep moving, wheeling my invalid beneath the gaze of a thickening crowd that I sense is very hostile, although I have no idea why. Hostile to her, hostile to me, hostile to the ill-starred, bothersome couple we make.

The dog keeps barking. I don't see the seated woman's face. She never turns round. The street has narrowed. We come abruptly to a point where it is being torn up. Men armed with shovels are digging ditches, others are using pickaxes to demolish the sidewalk. Our path is blocked. The dog barks louder and louder. I'm aware of the crowd behind me, unmoving, waiting. The street crew stops working to look at us. Some lean on their tools and snicker. I notice one man lighting a cigarette; another stoops, picks up a rock, and throws it in our direction. "They're going to stone us," says the invalid in a calm voice. They all drop their picks and shovels, stoop, pick up stones, and start throwing them. She turns around silently toward me, her face covered with blood. I scream and run back up the street, now empty.

In cities during the last century, a person on the verge of death was sheltered from noise. Straw was littered on the pavement outside his door to keep the wheels of carriages and stagecoaches off the resounding cobblestones. Evening strollers fell silent as they stepped across the straw, raising their eyes toward the curtained window from which faint light trickled. They knew that people there were sleeping, or keeping watch, or about to die.

Today no one knows anything.

What am I afraid of? Death? I know you, with your gaunt profile, taut ash-gray cheeks, hollow sockets, and enigmatic smiles. And I know you, glum effigies: your hair has lost its sheen and become heavy as clay; your fingers are brittle. I've never seen a dead woman. She'll be no different from you—very small and shrunken under the white sheet; her jaws clamped tight; stubborn; mysterious. Ugly, but beautiful to me. I'll take her hand in mine. No longer frightened of it.

My insidious and lamentable fear lies in the residue of life they want to offer me as a priceless gift, as their great achievement. Am I cowardly, and they deserving? I for being so shaken by living corruption, they for trying to resurrect a corpse? No one cares about her anymore, or whether she's longing to live or die. Listen, they say, it's not a question of longing but of will. You should think about the role of instinct, the wonderful instinct that animates all creation. If she hasn't died, it's because she wants to live. So we should let her live—no: *make* her. And I'm there to say thank you.

I see, from behind, a little girl whose curls, falling past her waist, are held in place by a blue velvet ribbon. Wrapped in a bathrobe, she's leaning against a door that opens on a December night. In one hand she holds a rag doll that drags on the floor; with the other she is waving a white handkerchief toward a fiacre that the night soon engulfs.

Whether crossing from bank to bank in a dark boat, or gliding from roof to treetop in nocturnal wandering, or gasping in anguish as we sleep in the Erlking's arms, we make our mysterious and dreaded "passage" sure of only one thing: we make it alone.

I lived in a waking dream. I thought I was helping her make her slow trek to the far side, holding the hand of a woman in danger to keep her from falling on the way and help her reach the slope of her last hill free of terror. Pure illusion. I thought I was at her side but she keeps escaping me. I see her crossing my horizon, but I can't make out the path she is taking.

I appointed myself warder of her memories, thinking I could take the place of her flooded brain and restock it with the living images it could no longer evoke. But I'm only an onlooker at a self-enclosed death agony. I know nothing about her now. Nothing, except this vacancy pierced by two unseeing eyes, and a heart that stubbornly goes on beating without respite.

My wayfarer, you have abandoned me outside a shuttered house whose walls are hung with crimson velvet, where antique clocks on marble mantels count seconds and chime hours, but where no hand is ever seen winding them up.

The sleepwalker wears a long diaphanous white dress that billows in the wind, her undone tresses stroke her waist, her invisible feet scarcely touch the roof gutter they walk on in the night. At a distance, she looks (in my myopic dreaming) blurred and diffuse. All at once the fluttering folds of tulle stiffen around her, her feet catch her hospital gown, and she falls.

I kept moving, I remember, I really had to, one foot in front of the other, like a robot. The smell was turning my stomach. The corridors of a morgue are always freezing; and the echo of steps is a compound of formalin and ice. Keep moving, go on, you have to see him. You have to see him dead, this first of your deaths. Yesterday he smiled at you. Go to him holding your pale pink rose, the kind he liked. What will be the color of his hands and brow?

A man in a gray smock stands waiting in front of an open door. That's the place. He takes me into a white-tiled, windowless room.

Along two opposite walls run huge cupboards like iceboxes with drawers set one above the other. One of the fluorescent bulbs in the ceiling will not light up completely and keeps blinking.

The man asks me, "Who do you want to see?" I tell him the name. After inspecting his ledger, he runs his finger along the drawers, peering through glasses in search of the number. He beckons to me. Pulling out the drawer, he turns back the sheet and uncovers a face. It's not him. I say, "It's not him." "You sure?" he replies in astonishment. Reluctantly, he covers the face, closes the drawer, and returns to his register. He comes back shrugging his shoulders. It was one drawer over. He pulls it open; he reveals the face. It's him: my brother. Asleep in a suburban cupboard. That's where he ended up. All alone. Mummified in a deep freeze. My lips touch his forehead. Stone. I place the rose under his chin. There was a purplish stain across the nape of his neck that I'll never forget. Something burst there, and blood spread under the skin. While he was going under without a murmur. I cover the faintly smiling face and disheveled black hair. The drawer closes. "Thank you," I say to the man, "good-bye, Monsieur," handing him a bill that he hurriedly stuffs into a pocket. It's sunny outside.

I'm walking through the rooms of a museum peopled with shadows. Is it dark because I'm asleep and know it's nighttime? Or are these shapes I happen to see emerging from a deeper night that I'm not allowed to enter?

Down the dimly lit museum corridors comes a hackneyed song—a popular waltz tune that used to make people cry. Sung tonight by a rasping voice, dimly pounded out on a faraway pianola. "*C'est aujourd'hui dimanche . . .*" (later, there are *roses blanches*). A poor sad song, now it's gotten stuck at the third measure, it repeats itself over and over in the silence, until it is at last transformed—one two three, dum de dum—into the Chopin waltz whose name I've forgotten. It's coming closer. At the turning point of a corridor the city glow faintly illuminates a small circular room, above which a glass dome reveals the stars. At the center of the room stands a piano. From it (dum de dum) the little waltz is pouring forth.

Falling from an invisible spotlight, a medallion of blue light is poised on the pianist's face. Her torso is motionless, stiff within the black velvet of her dress. Nothing moves except her lips, which seem stitched in black on the blue face. They are contorted as they articulate the words of an inaudible song. I go nearer and see, resting on the keyboard whose keys rise and fall without their touching them, two hands that are fleshless, stiff, and paralyzed.

The sixth of December is the feast of St. Nicholas. Each year she'd have Edelmann, the Strasbourg confectioner, send her chocolate-and-gingerbread effigies of the saint, which she'd distribute among the children. This year Madame Edelmann will say to her husband, "Strange—the woman, *weisst du*, the one who's always written to us, from way back, *so lange her*—she didn't write this year. Maybe she died, *wer weiss*? *Die arme Frau*!"

When she was fed up with it, she would drop her knitting into the workbasket and start embroidering, using the round wooden embroidery frame attached to one armrest of her chair. When she was fed up with embroidery, she would push away the frame, grab her cane, stand up with a more or less successful lunge, and take three steps over to the oval table, where she would settle on a chair.

A deck of cards lay on the loosely knit wool tablecloth. She would straighten her glasses on her nose, pick up the deck with her left hand, and lay out the cards for a game of solitaire. She was capable of spending hours this way, laying out the cards, picking them up, laying them out again. Knitting, embroidery, solitaire. The days passed.

She dreaded becoming senile. One day I found a bottle of sleeping pills hidden in the lining of her workbasket.

And the night at dinner when she began crying, sobbing like a little girl because I had pointed out some food that stuck to the corner of her mouth.

It's early, always very early, when everyone is asleep and the city is in a state of lethargy, that hospitals get rid of their dead. Outside the morgue, a black car waits for sullen men to finish screwing down the wooden coffin lid.

This will happen to you, too, and flowers will conceal the oak and the chrome plaque on which your name has been engraved in fine sloping letters.

In pale yellow light at the far end of a hallway, I see a woman lying in a coffin. She looks peacefully asleep on her lace pillow, held snugly in place by the white satin quilting. Next to her, stiff as a statue, the guardian of the place stands watch. His heavyset frame is trussed in a white smock. With one huge cold-reddened hand he holds the other, which is shaking uncontrollably. A nervous tic distorts his right cheek, pulling his slack mouth upward. He has the face of a total idiot. Here where he has been stationed, he can frighten no one.

He must have been the one who tenderly dressed the dead woman in her evening gown (pearl-gray highlighted with threads of silver); whose coarse hands so delicately made her up (the foundation still intact, pale rouge on the cheekbones, lipstick on the parted lips); who arranged her hair and threaded a little amber rosary between her diaphanous fingers.

I shall encounter her by chance one day between a museum's barest walls. I won't be surprised. She will be sitting there, motionless in her gloomy surroundings, as if she had been expecting me for years. I shall go up to her. Gradually the white walls around us will fade away, and I shall see her in the dull glow of the floor lamp that stands beside her.

Stretched out on the bed in her waxy old clothes, her white hands folded across her breast, she will not have changed. Inside the jar that forms her skull the sockets will be hollow. The young woman in the round portrait may be smiling, but the jars around the neck are empty.

Above the bed, in his oval frame, the dear departed looks as displeased as ever, and against the woman's bony legs a fat gray cat lies curled.

The phone is ringing. It's cold. The window is wide open. It will be morning soon.

The phone is ringing. "Madame, I'm sorry. You have to wake up." (Periwinkle's gentle voice.) "Madame, you must come back. Your mother is dead."

MARIE CHAIX, born in Lyons and raised in Paris, is the author of nine books, including *The Laurels of Lake Constance* (Dalkey Archive, 2012). *The Summer of the Elder Tree*, a memoir and meditation on the theme of separation, and her first book in more than a decade, was published in Paris in 2005, and will appear from Dalkey Archive Press in 2013.

HARRY MATHEWS has written over a dozen books including the novels *Cigarettes* and *Tlooth*, along with his collected essays, *The Case of the Persevering Maltese*. Mathews is a member of the Oulipo—France's longest-lived and most active literary group. He divides his time between Paris, Key West, and New York.

SELECTED DALKEY ARCHIVE TITLES

Michal Ajvaz, *The Golden Age.*
The Other City.
Pierre Albert-Birot, *Grabinoulor.*
Yuz Aleshkovsky, *Kangaroo.*
Felipe Alfau, *Chromos.*
Locos.
Ivan Ângelo, *The Celebration.*
The Tower of Glass.
António Lobo Antunes, *Knowledge of Hell.*
The Splendor of Portugal.
Alain Arias-Misson, *Theatre of Incest.*
John Ashbery and James Schuyler, *A Nest of Ninnies.*
Robert Ashley, *Perfect Lives.*
Gabriela Avigur-Rotem, *Heatwave and Crazy Birds.*
Djuna Barnes, *Ladies Almanack.*
Ryder.
John Barth, *LETTERS.*
Sabbatical.
Donald Barthelme, *The King.*
Paradise.
Svetislav Basara, *Chinese Letter.*
Miquel Bauçà, *The Siege in the Room.*
René Belletto, *Dying.*
Marek Bieńczyk, *Transparency.*
Andrei Bitov, *Pushkin House.*
Andrej Blatnik, *You Do Understand.*
Louis Paul Boon, *Chapel Road.*
My Little War.
Summer in Termuren.
Roger Boylan, *Killoyle.*
Ignácio de Loyola Brandão, *Anonymous Celebrity.*
Zero.
Bonnie Bremser, *Troia: Mexican Memoirs.*
Christine Brooke-Rose, *Amalgamemnon.*
Brigid Brophy, *In Transit.*
Gerald L. Bruns, *Modern Poetry and the Idea of Language.*
Gabrielle Burton, *Heartbreak Hotel.*
Michel Butor, *Degrees.*
Mobile.
G. Cabrera Infante, *Infante's Inferno.*
Three Trapped Tigers.
Julieta Campos, *The Fear of Losing Eurydice.*
Anne Carson, *Eros the Bittersweet.*
Orly Castel-Bloom, *Dolly City.*
Louis-Ferdinand Céline, *Castle to Castle.*
Conversations with Professor Y.
London Bridge.
Normance.
North.
Rigadoon.
Marie Chaix, *The Laurels of Lake Constance.*
Hugo Charteris, *The Tide Is Right.*
Eric Chevillard, *Demolishing Nisard.*
Marc Cholodenko, *Mordechai Schamz.*
Joshua Cohen, *Witz.*
Emily Holmes Coleman, *The Shutter of Snow.*
Robert Coover, *A Night at the Movies.*
Stanley Crawford, *Log of the S.S. The Mrs Unguentine.*
Some Instructions to My Wife.
René Crevel, *Putting My Foot in It.*
Ralph Cusack, *Cadenza.*
Nicholas Delbanco, *The Count of Concord.*
Sherbrookes.
Nigel Dennis, *Cards of Identity.*
Peter Dimock, *A Short Rhetoric for Leaving the Family.*
Ariel Dorfman, *Konfidenz.*
Coleman Dowell, *Island People.*
Too Much Flesh and Jabez.
Arkadii Dragomoshchenko, *Dust.*
Rikki Ducornet, *The Complete Butcher's Tales.*
The Fountains of Neptune.
The Jade Cabinet.
Phosphor in Dreamland.
William Eastlake, *The Bamboo Bed.*
Castle Keep.
Lyric of the Circle Heart.
Jean Echenoz, *Chopin's Move.*
Stanley Elkin, *A Bad Man.*
Criers and Kibitzers, Kibitzers and Criers.
The Dick Gibson Show.
The Franchiser.
The Living End.
Mrs. Ted Bliss.
François Emmanuel, *Invitation to a Voyage.*
Salvador Espriu, *Ariadne in the Grotesque Labyrinth.*
Leslie A. Fiedler, *Love and Death in the American Novel.*
Juan Filloy, *Op Oloop.*
Andy Fitch, *Pop Poetics.*
Gustave Flaubert, *Bouvard and Pécuchet.*
Kass Fleisher, *Talking out of School.*
Ford Madox Ford, *The March of Literature.*
Jon Fosse, *Aliss at the Fire.*
Melancholy.
Max Frisch, *I'm Not Stiller.*
Man in the Holocene.
Carlos Fuentes, *Christopher Unborn.*
Distant Relations.
Terra Nostra.
Where the Air Is Clear.
Takehiko Fukunaga, *Flowers of Grass.*
William Gaddis, *J R.*
The Recognitions.
Janice Galloway, *Foreign Parts.*
The Trick Is to Keep Breathing.
William H. Gass, *Cartesian Sonata and Other Novellas.*
Finding a Form.
A Temple of Texts.
The Tunnel.
Willie Masters' Lonesome Wife.
Gérard Gavarry, *Hoppla! 1 2 3.*
Etienne Gilson, *The Arts of the Beautiful.*
Forms and Substances in the Arts.
C. S. Giscombe, *Giscome Road.*
Here.
Douglas Glover, *Bad News of the Heart.*
Witold Gombrowicz, *A Kind of Testament.*
Paulo Emílio Sales Gomes, *P's Three Women.*
Georgi Gospodinov, *Natural Novel.*
Juan Goytisolo, *Count Julian.*
Juan the Landless.
Makbara.
Marks of Identity.

FOR A FULL LIST OF PUBLICATIONS, VISIT:
www.dalkeyarchive.com

SELECTED DALKEY ARCHIVE TITLES

SELECTED DALKEY ARCHIVE TITLES

The Princess Hoppy.
Some Thing Black.
LEON S. ROUDIEZ, *French Fiction Revisited.*
RAYMOND ROUSSEL, *Impressions of Africa.*
VEDRANA RUDAN, *Night.*
STIG SÆTERBAKKEN, *Siamese.*
LYDIE SALVAYRE, *The Company of Ghosts.*
Everyday Life.
The Lecture.
Portrait of the Writer as a Domesticated Animal.
The Power of Flies.
LUIS RAFAEL SÁNCHEZ, *Macho Camacho's Beat.*
SEVERO SARDUY, *Cobra & Maitreya.*
NATHALIE SARRAUTE, *Do You Hear Them?*
Martereau.
The Planetarium.
ARNO SCHMIDT, *Collected Novellas.*
Collected Stories.
Nobodaddy's Children.
Two Novels.
ASAF SCHURR, *Motti.*
CHRISTINE SCHUTT, *Nightwork.*
GAIL SCOTT, *My Paris.*
DAMION SEARLS, *What We Were Doing and Where We Were Going.*
JUNE AKERS SEESE, *Is This What Other Women Feel Too?*
What Waiting Really Means.
BERNARD SHARE, *Inish.*
Transit.
AURELIE SHEEHAN, *Jack Kerouac Is Pregnant.*
VIKTOR SHKLOVSKY, *Bowstring.*
Knight's Move.
A Sentimental Journey: Memoirs 1917–1922.
Energy of Delusion: A Book on Plot.
Literature and Cinematography.
Theory of Prose.
Third Factory.
Zoo, or Letters Not about Love.
CLAUDE SIMON, *The Invitation.*
PIERRE SINIAC, *The Collaborators.*
KJERSTI A. SKOMSVOLD, *The Faster I Walk, the Smaller I Am.*
JOSEF ŠKVORECKÝ, *The Engineer of Human Souls.*
GILBERT SORRENTINO, *Aberration of Starlight.*
Blue Pastoral.
Crystal Vision.
Imaginative Qualities of Actual Things.
Mulligan Stew.
Pack of Lies.
Red the Fiend.
The Sky Changes.
Something Said.
Splendide-Hôtel.
Steelwork.
Under the Shadow.
W. M. SPACKMAN, *The Complete Fiction.*
ANDRZEJ STASIUK, *Dukla.*
Fado.
GERTRUDE STEIN, *Lucy Church Amiably.*
The Making of Americans.
A Novel of Thank You.
LARS SVENDSEN, *A Philosophy of Evil.*
PIOTR SZEWC, *Annihilation.*
GONÇALO M. TAVARES, *Jerusalem.*
Joseph Walser's Machine.
Learning to Pray in the Age of Technique.
LUCIAN DAN TEODOROVICI, *Our Circus Presents . . .*
NIKANOR TERATOLOGEN, *Assisted Living.*
STEFAN THEMERSON, *Hobson's Island.*
The Mystery of the Sardine.
Tom Harris.
TAEKO TOMIOKA, *Building Waves.*
JOHN TOOMEY, *Sleepwalker.*
JEAN-PHILIPPE TOUSSAINT, *The Bathroom.*
Camera.
Monsieur.
Reticence.
Running Away.
Self-Portrait Abroad.
Television.
The Truth about Marie.
DUMITRU TSEPENEAG, *Hotel Europa.*
The Necessary Marriage.
Pigeon Post.
Vain Art of the Fugue.
ESTHER TUSQUETS, *Stranded.*
DUBRAVKA UGRESIC, *Lend Me Your Character.*
Thank You for Not Reading.
TOR ULVEN, *Replacement.*
MATI UNT, *Brecht at Night.*
Diary of a Blood Donor.
Things in the Night.
ÁLVARO URIBE AND OLIVIA SEARS, EDS., *Best of Contemporary Mexican Fiction.*
ELOY URROZ, *Friction.*
The Obstacles.
LUISA VALENZUELA, *Dark Desires and the Others.*
He Who Searches.
MARJA-LIISA VARTIO, *The Parson's Widow.*
PAUL VERHAEGHEN, *Omega Minor.*
AGLAJA VETERANYI, *Why the Child Is Cooking in the Polenta.*
BORIS VIAN, *Heartsnatcher.*
LLORENÇ VILLALONGA, *The Dolls' Room.*
TOOMAS VINT, *An Unending Landscape.*
ORNELA VORPSI, *The Country Where No One Ever Dies.*
AUSTRYN WAINHOUSE, *Hedyphagetica.*
PAUL WEST, *Words for a Deaf Daughter & Gala.*
CURTIS WHITE, *America's Magic Mountain.*
The Idea of Home.
Memories of My Father Watching TV.
Monstrous Possibility: An Invitation to Literary Politics.
Requiem.
DIANE WILLIAMS, *Excitability: Selected Stories.*
Romancer Erector.
DOUGLAS WOOLF, *Wall to Wall.*
Ya! & John-Juan.
JAY WRIGHT, *Polynomials and Pollen.*
The Presentable Art of Reading Absence.
PHILIP WYLIE, *Generation of Vipers.*
MARGUERITE YOUNG, *Angel in the Forest.*
Miss MacIntosh, My Darling.
REYOUNG, *Unbabbling.*
VLADO ŽABOT, *The Succubus.*
ZORAN ŽIVKOVIĆ, *Hidden Camera.*
LOUIS ZUKOFSKY, *Collected Fiction.*
VITOMIL ZUPAN, *Minuet for Guitar.*
SCOTT ZWIREN, *God Head.*

FOR A FULL LIST OF PUBLICATIONS, VISIT:
www.dalkeyarchive.com